"I don't even know how long I'll be in town."

The sadness in Abigail's voice urged Hudson to ask her who abandoned her as a kid. He hated that his heart twisted at the thought of her leaving. He needed to change the subject. "There's been something bothering me since this morning. You had another one of your extreme reactions around another De La Rosa."

He moved closer to her. Close enough to see every detail of her reaction when he asked his question. "Do you have some sort of connection with the family I should know about?"

He tended to follow his instincts, and they were screaming that she was hiding something important.

She blinked, like a deer frozen in the middle of the road, staring into the headlights. She was panicking. She was deciding how much of the truth to tell him, if any.

Leaning a hip on the table, he crossed his arms and stared at her, stone-faced. Letting her know without a word that he was not letting this go until he had the truth.

A seventh-generation Texan, **Jolene Navarro** fills her life with family, faith and life's beautiful messiness. She knows that as much as the world changes, people stay the same: vow-keepers and heartbreakers. Jolene married a vow-keeper who shows her holding hands never gets old. When not writing, Jolene teaches art to teens and hangs out with her own four almost-grown kids. Find Jolene on Facebook or her blog, jolenenavarrowriter.com.

Books by Jolene Navarro

Love Inspired

Cowboys of Diamondback Ranch

The Texan's Secret Daughter
The Texan's Surprise Return
The Texan's Promise
The Texan's Unexpected Holiday
The Texan's Truth
Her Holiday Secret
Claiming Her Texas Family

Lone Star Legacy

Texas Daddy
The Texan's Twins
Lone Star Christmas

Visit the Author Profile page at LoveInspired.com for more titles.

Claiming Her Texas Family

Jolene Navarro

LOVE INSPIRED
INSPIRATIONAL ROMANCE

LOVE INSPIRED®
INSPIRATIONAL ROMANCE

ISBN-13: 978-1-335-58515-8

Claiming Her Texas Family

Love Inspired
22 Adelaide St. West, 41st Floor
Toronto, Ontario M5H 4E3, Canada
www.LoveInspired.com

Printed in U.S.A.

Let your conversation be without covetousness;
and be content with such things as ye have:
for he hath said, I will never leave thee,
nor forsake thee. So that we may boldly say,
The Lord is my helper, and I will not fear
what man shall do unto me.
                    —*Hebrews* 13:5–6

Last year Texas went through an unprecedented winter storm. For the first time in recorded history, every county was covered in ice and snow. Without the resources and equipment to handle that type of natural disaster, first responders and many others stepped up and did what they could for their community. The needs varied, but they all demonstrated the resilience of the human spirit with bravery and hope. Thank you.

Chapter One

A strong January wind pushed at Abigail Dixon's Mercedes as she crossed the bridge from the mainland. Releasing a breath, she turned onto Shoreline Drive. The small coastal town of Port Del Mar, Texas, was a quaint mix of brightly painted stores, weatherworn buildings and blurry childhood memories.

She checked her rearview mirror, then narrowed her eyes. Was that the same black truck she saw this morning crossing into Texas? She had never seen a vehicle like it before. It was some sort of mix between a Jeep and a monster truck. Her fingers involuntarily tightened around the steering wheel. Had a reporter already found her?

Shaking her head, she forced herself to relax. Being paranoid was new for her, but after the last year, maybe it wasn't so ridiculous.

Back in Cincinnati, she hadn't been able to leave her house due to reporters shouting questions and all the angry people just spewing hatred. They believed she was as guilty as her ex-husband. Their outrage was justified, but she had been just as betrayed by Brady.

Tamping down those thoughts, she focused on the new life she was going to build. Brady was her past, but God used everything for good. Her ex-husband had given her the most precious gift. Her nine-month-old daughter.

It was a true blessing that Paloma was too young to remember any of the drama her father had brought into their lives. This would be a clean start—and Abigail would be smarter this time.

Paloma whimpered from the back seat.

"Shh, baby girl. It's going to be okay." Her sweet daughter was here because of her three-year marriage to Brady. She would do it all again for Paloma.

"I promise you will always have me, no matter what."

The goal now was to find a safe place where she could regroup and have time to lay out a plan for their future. Maybe she would take her real family's name again. Abigail released a sigh.

De La Rosa was a pretty name, and they had a ranch here on the coast of Texas. The Diamondback Ranch was her last chance to reconnect with that family. But what if they still didn't want her?

She checked the rearview mirror again. The suspicious vehicle was still there. Could someone be tracking her down? The family ranch was miles past the middle of nowhere. If she kept driving, she would be alone with Paloma, completely vulnerable.

And after all these years Abigail didn't know anything about her family, other than that they owned the Diamondback Ranch and she was the youngest. Or she *had* been when they'd sent her to live with her great-aunt after her mother's death. Was her father remarried with new kids?

Forcing air into her lungs, she let it out slowly and relaxed each tense muscle, one by one.

Her aunt had taken her as soon as her mother's funeral was over. She had just turned nine.

To say that her mother's aunt had hated her father would be a huge understatement. The older woman had used every opportunity to make sure Abigail understood she was better off without the horrid family that had ruined her poor mother.

She'd waited for her family to come for her. But her father hadn't even called, not once. No letters either. She had hung on to hope, but none of them had reached out to her. Would he turn his back on her and his granddaughter?

But if she didn't go to the ranch, where would she go? She was technically homeless.

Blinking back the tears burning her eyes, she gripped the steering wheel. She didn't have time to cry or feel sorry for herself. Now that she was here, her insides heaved at the thought of facing her family.

Slowing down, she scanned the four lanes of the main street. The beach wall was on her left. There were parallel parking spots with meters. But since that car was still on her tail, those were too visible.

On her right was a line of stores and restaurants. It being off-season, there weren't many people. Abigail parked in the middle of the strip, between two big trucks jacked up for off-roading. The tires were taller than her car. They gave her an odd sense of protection.

In front of her was Hope Family Health and Birthing Center that had the look of an inviting cottage, smack in the middle of businesses. At the far end, a bakery stood out with bold colors. A pink sign trimmed in turquoise and orange read Dulce Panadería in elegant script.

Clusters of ornate tables with empty chairs under a pergola, begged people to slow down and sit. Bright paper banners and café lights trimmed the area. It looked like a cupcake waiting for a party.

The store had more of a fun Mexican fiesta vibe than a Texas coastal one. A tiny woman was sweeping the little patio area. She frowned at the sky, then disappeared back into the shop.

Abigail glanced around. Should she go in? This indecisiveness had to stop. Rolling her shoulders, she took a deep breath and held it before releasing it slowly. Finally, ready, she swung open the car door and was hit by a cold bitter January wind.

Dark glasses and hat in place, Abigail pushed herself out of the car.

Another gust of freezing air took her breath and seared her throat. Texas should not be this cold. It wasn't in her memories—but then again, she had been so young when they'd sent her away. Bundling her baby in her warm blanket, she lifted her out of her car seat and pulled her close. Diaper bag swung over her shoulder and head high, she moved away from her little red Mercedes. It was the only thing she still owned. Everything else was gone. She needed to trade it in for something more practical and less obvious.

A cup of coffee would help her figure out her next move. Gathering information about her family before knocking on their door would probably be the smart thing to do. And could also save her a lot of heartache.

She glanced around as though she were a spy hiding from dangerous people. The problem was that she obviously didn't know how to spot the people who were bad for her. Brady Dixon was strong evidence on that front. What about her family? According to her aunt, they were the worst of the worst.

The wasps that had nested in her gut released their stingers. Reaching for the bottle of antacids in her purse, she nearly cried to find it was empty. She was too young to be living on this stuff.

The town was small. The woman in the shop had to know the De La Rosa family. Hopefully she would be able to give her some information. Showing up at the ranch without knowing what she was walking into wasn't much better than hiding in Cincinnati.

It's not like they would recognize her anyway. Her nickname had been Chunky Monkey, but the chunk had disappeared, along with the talkative hyper kid begging for attention.

At nine, her hair had been dark, almost black, and it had hung past her waist in a long braid. Her mother would plait it every morning. Now it was in a sharp, angled cut and platinum blond.

The right side of her hair fell over her eye. With a shaking hand, she tried to tuck it behind her ear. Brady had liked it this way. She should let it grow out and maybe go back to being a brunette.

A sweet, happy bell chimed when she opened the door to the *panadería*. Sugar, cinnamon and baked apples mixed with the rich aroma of coffee made her stomach rumble.

Fresh flowers of every color were gathered in a variety of vintage bottles and there were small shelves scattered around with all sorts of books. It had all the feel of coming home. The way she imagined it, anyway.

The woman who had been outside slipped in behind the counter. "Buenos días! Welcome to Port Del Mar. What can I get for you this morning?"

People this happy made her suspicious. Abigail took her time studying the handwritten menu on the chalkboard. In her peripheral vision, she glimpsed the black monster truck she had seen several times pulling into the spot in front of the bakery. Her lungs stopped.

A tall brick wall of a man stepped out of the vehicle and scanned both directions of the sidewalk before moving forward—into the bakery.

He *was* following her. Was there an emergency exit?

"Are you okay, *mija*?" the woman leaned across the counter and rested her hand on Abigail's arm.

"I think that man is following me. I know it sounds—"

"Josefina!" The woman called over her shoulder. "We might have trouble."

"Oh no. I'm probably overreacting." Abigail waved her hand to waylay the shopkeeper. She was being ridiculous and now was making a scene. "I'm sorry. Please don't—"

"It's okay. If you feel threatened, we'll work it out." She looked at the slightly taller woman who had emerged from the back. They were so much alike they could be twins. "Call Bridges."

The woman glanced back at Abigail. "I'm Margarita. This is my sister Josefina Espinoza, and she's calling our brother. He's a cop," she whispered as she leaned forward.

The two women came out from behind the counter to stand in front of her. Josefina was casually holding the largest cast-iron skillet Abigail had ever seen.

The sisters were shorter than her, but each stood at one of her shoulders, defending her. They didn't know anything about her. It would be so much easier if she just slipped out the back. And go where? Her life was at a dead end.

The bell chimed. It didn't sound happy this time. A gust of cold air pushed its way into the warm, cozy shop.

The man stopped. He was an intimidating male well over six feet tall. Abigail wasn't sure they could do much damage if he decided to try something. Even three against one the odds were not good.

Both women relaxed. Margarita gave her arm a squeeze, then stepped forward with a big grin on her face. "Sheriff Menchaca, what are you doing running around scaring innocent women?"

Sheriff? He was the sheriff? That should have reassured her, but a new dread slithered through her veins. She was not at all confident that she would fare any better with the law. Her experience with them hadn't been all that great.

He quirked one eyebrow and removed his cowboy hat. "Innocent women have nothing to fear from me. I just stopped in for my coffee and empanada." He ran his hands through dark, thick hair that had been pressed down by the hat. His gaze shifted to Abigail. "Is there a problem?"

Lifting her chin to make eye contact, she stifled a gasp. His eyes. One was a liquid gold and the other an indigo blue. Aware she was staring; she shifted her gaze down. Twisting her head to look at her daughter, she watched him from the corner of her vision.

His gaze darted between the three women, stopping on Abigail.

If he learned about the crimes in Cincinnati, would he think she was guilty like everyone else? Maybe they had called ahead and warned him. Did they do that? Was that the reason he was following her?

Those gold-blue eyes were staring at her. After a moment of silence, he lowered his chin, but his gaze stayed steady. Unsettled, she shifted her daughter to her other shoulder.

"I…um." She cleared her throat. "Were you following me?"

"Should I be?" Was that amusement pulling at the corner of his lips? The dark skin and lines at his eyes made it clear that this man didn't sit behind a desk often.

Abigail looked behind her. There was a back exit not far from where they stood.

"Sheriff, let me get your favorite coffee." Margarita nudged him to the counter, but he didn't budge.

The two sisters had jumped in because she was scared. No one had ever stood up for her just because she had asked. Maybe this could be a place she could stay, for a few days at least. She was so tired of running.

"Ma'am?" His gaze narrowed as he studied her as if she was a problem to be solved. "Are you all right?"

His voice invited a person to sit and listen to his every word. But she couldn't afford to be lured in by another charming man.

With one step he was just a few feet from her. "Is there someone I can call for you?"

The sheriff reached out and gently touched her arm. Out of instinct, she jerked away from his touch. The diaper bag slipped off her shoulder and fell to the floor.

Abigail had been in the car for over twenty hours. She probably looked questionable, and he had every right to be concerned. But not a single word could be formed in her brain. She was exhausted.

"I'm sorry. I didn't mean to startle you." Without being asked, he dropped to his haunches in front of her and gathered her spilled items.

Well, that was a novelty. She didn't know any man who would take the blame and apologize so quickly. She wasn't even sure it was his fault.

Straightening, he took a step back and held out her bag.

Not sure what to do, she just stared at the bag.

"Ma'am. Let me call someone for you," he offered again.

Tears burned her eyes. There was no one to call. She was so alone. Without meeting his gaze, she took the bag.

Brady had been all charming at first, too. He said he would take care of her. The first year, he'd made her feel like she was the most important person in his world, but then they got married and it all changed. She had become just one more of his prized treasures to show off.

That part of her life was over. This was her chance to reinvent herself one more time. She gently bounced Paloma. Now the stakes were higher. It wasn't just her life that was impacted.

Take a deep breath. Smile. Be normal. She couldn't afford to lose control. *Pull it together.*

"What's wrong?" The sheriff had kept his distance during her little mental freak-out, but he didn't look happy about it.

With everything in place, she looked back up. "Thank you, but I'm good."

His eyes squinted as he tilted his head and scrutinized her face, doubt all over his handsome features.

Her daughter whimpered, then cried out. Abigail's heart rate spiked. Something was wrong. Had her run to Texas just put her daughter in more danger?

Chapter Two

Warning flags of every color were flying in Hudson's head. The young mother looked like she was about to bolt. Instead of following Margarita's subtle suggestion, he held his hand up to calm her. That was a rookie move.

He quickly adjusted and turned his palms up, indicating that he had nothing to hide. Then he relaxed his mouth into a smile so that he would be less intimidating. He was very aware that his size could be scary to someone that didn't know him. It was an asset in his role as sheriff, but it didn't help in situations like this.

Margarita's lips curved in a friendly expression, but her eyes were telling him to move on. Josefina stood shoulder to shoulder with the woman. He had to grin at their protectiveness.

He towered over them, but they didn't seem to notice. Somehow, they managed to look down on him. That was a true talent, since he was six foot three. The Espinoza sisters might be small, but they were fierce. No wonder their brother was one of his best deputies.

Narrowing his eyes, Hudson studied the newcomer again. She was small in a frail type of way. Like she hadn't eaten well in a long time. Her nearly black eyes were too big for her face, and her golden brown skin had an unnatural pallor. And there was nothing natural about the slick blond hair that followed the line of her jaw.

Something was off. She was either scared or guilty. He couldn't figure out which one. Yet.

His first instinct was to jump in and protect her, but that had gotten him in trouble before. The thing that threatened to tear at his heart was the way she was holding her baby girl close, protecting her child. Yeah, that got him every time. A mother protecting her child was his weakness.

He couldn't afford any weaknesses. Port Del Mar was a new beginning for him and his daughter.

This woman was a walking contradiction, and he didn't like unknowns. Only six months ago, the people of Port Del Mar had voted him in as their new sheriff without really knowing him. They had taken the word of his military buddy, Xavier De La Rosa, that he'd be a good fit for the community. But they were watching his every move and still deciding if their trust had been placed in the right hands.

So, there was a good chance he was overreacting. Yet firsthand experience had taught him that an innocent-looking woman could cause the most damage when he let his guard down.

"Do you have a name?" he asked, making sure to keep his voice soft and as nonthreatening as possible.

Her eyes went wide for a second, then she blinked. If he hadn't been staring, he might have missed the flash of panic.

Her daughter cried out, and her head jerked down.

With a soothing sound, she bounced the baby. He assumed the baby was a girl, as she was bundled in pink.

"Come on, Sheriff." Margarita coaxed him to the counter again. "I'll make you the perfect coffee for this cold morning."

This time he allowed the oldest Espinoza to lead him away. "Did she give you a name before you went to battle for her?" he asked.

Margarita ignored him as she fixed his coffee. Leaning against the counter on one elbow, he turned to keep his gaze on the stranger.

They made eye contact, and this time she didn't look away. Instead, she lifted her chin. The corner of his mouth pulled up.

Her eyes narrowed. That only made his grin spread wider. It was all he could do not to chuckle outright at her fierceness. But those large, obsidian irises couldn't totally hide the fear.

He took a step forward, then stopped.

She *was* just a job. He had taken an oath to protect this sleepy beachside town, and his gut told him there was a problem here. Either she was trouble, or the trouble was following her here.

He popped his jaw and rolled his shoulders he tried to relax the muscles. The more obstacles she put up, the harder it was for him to let this go. But logically he knew she was probably just as she appeared. A single mother traveling with a baby. Maybe there had been a bad breakup and she needed a new start.

But why a Texas beach town so small most folks didn't know it was here? If the unfamiliar car in front of the clinic was hers, she was from Ohio. Driving a thousand miles alone with a baby couldn't be easy. Was she running from someone?

He narrowed his eyes at her again. His gut told him she was hiding something. And he wasn't leaving until he had a few simple questions answered.

It didn't take a PhD to know why he was driven to save women. Even the ones that didn't need or want saving.

The bell chimed, warning of someone new entering the bakery. A tall male walked into the store as if he belonged there. It was Margarita and Josefina's brother, his deputy, Bridges Espinoza.

Hudson nodded. "Espinoza."

"Bridges!" the sisters said in cheerful unison.

"What took you so long?" Margarita chided.

Josefina jumped in on top of her. "We could have been in real trouble by now."

Bridges scanned the area. "You called the sheriff too?" His gaze came back to Hudson. "What's going on?"

He shrugged, not sure why they had called their brother. "I just came in for coffee and an empanada."

Margarita interrupted. "We thought we might need backup, but we handled it." She pushed Hudson's coffee across the counter and went back to make one for her brother.

"This poor woman and her baby were all alone and scared." Josefina pulled out a chair and motioned the still unnamed woman to sit. "She thought someone was stalking her, but it turned out to be the sheriff. It took you a long time to get here." She gave her brother a disapproving frown.

"I'm not always in town. Which is why in a real

emergency you need to call 911." He turned to Hudson. "I was out on the De La Rosa ranch."

"Any problem I should be aware of?" he asked.

"Naw. Belle called me just to have a look. There were some downed fences, evidence of trespassing. Probably bored teens. Not much to do this time of year. More important question—" Bridges tipped his coffee to him "—why were you stalking this woman?" True confusion coated his words.

A tinge of irritation tweaked at him that the De La Rosas had not called him. Even though they had elected him as sheriff, the town still acted as if they didn't completely trust him with local issues. "I wasn't. I was just following my normal routine." Why was he explaining himself?

Coffee in hand, Hudson turned from his deputy and approached the woman again. "Can I sit?" He indicated a chair opposite her.

She nodded and shifted the now fussy baby to her other shoulder.

Hudson glanced at the chalkboard wall. He turned to the woman. "Can I get you something?"

At first, she shook her head, lips pulled tight. Then she sighed and bounced the baby. "Josefina is bringing me a hot chocolate, but thank you." With her free hand, she dug into the bag on her shoulder and pulled out a half-full bottle. Offering it to her daughter, she kept her head down.

"You thought I was stalking you? Is there a reason you suspect someone was following you?" Slowly, he studied her features.

"I'm sure I was overreacting."

"Can you at least give me your name? I can help if you need it."

Her gaze shot up to his as if in surprise. "I'm… Abigail Dixon." She looked as if that should mean something. "And I appreciate the offer, but I'll be fine."

He let her name roll around in his head. It didn't click with anyone he knew. "Abigail Dixon. If that's your car with the Ohio plates, you're far from home. Traveling alone with a baby can't be easy."

She released a deep sigh. "No." Her face tightened, and she turned away from him to look at her baby. Her petite shoulders rose and fell with several deep breaths.

Something was wrong. The trouble might be *her* after all. Shifting back in his chair, he looked over her shoulder. "Sure, I can't help you?"

Her mouth pursed as her gaze darted around the room. With another heavy sigh, she finally made eye contact with him. "I might as well tell you. It wouldn't take much for you to find out anyway. I left Ohio to get away from the trouble my ex-husband caused. I want a clean start, so I'd appreciate it if that information stayed between you and me."

There was another long pause. Worst-case scenarios ricocheted through his brain.

"You might have heard of him. My ex-husband," she mumbled, hiding her gaze.

Not being able to hear, he was forced to lean closer. The soft scent of cucumbers and wildflowers teased him. Her eyes met his, and they both stilled, neither willing to break the contact. "What is it? Is it something I can help with?" Yeah, he was an idiot.

She shook her head. "Brady Dixon. He's in a federal prison for grand theft and fraud."

Whoa. The back of the chair stopped him from falling. Brady Dixon had stolen millions of dollars of innocent people's money. It had been big enough to make the national news. Hudson blinked. That man had lived the high life by taking other people's dreams. He had seen images of yachts, private planes and luxury cars. She had been living that lifestyle? The red Mercedes parked out front made more sense now. The most luxurious thing in his little coastal town was the De La Rosas' fake pirate ship.

"You were married to Brady Dixon?"

Pressing her full lips into a firm line, she shifted her gaze to the side. "I was. Not anymore."

His gut twisted. Why was she here?

She cleared her throat and tried to soothe her fussy baby. "Since you're the sheriff, you might need to know in case reporters show up or something. But as I said, I would prefer to keep it between us." She leaned forward as much as the baby would allow. "I came to Port Del Mar hoping to disappear and start anew. Yes, I was married to Brady Dixon. Yes, he is now in federal prison for grand larceny and fraud. Yes, I was investigated too, but I was never charged."

He considered her for a moment, studying the details of her features. Was there something he was missing? "I've heard of the case." Starting over somewhere new he could understand. "Why all the way down here? How did you even find Port Del Mar?"

"Would you believe me if I told you I threw a dart at a map of the US?" The baby fussed again.

"A dart brought you to Port Del Mar, Texas? Population 378 during the off-season? I'm not sure we would even be on the map."

Swaying her baby, she shrugged.

He couldn't help but ask because she was in his town. As the sheriff, he had a right to know. "You really had no clue where he was getting his money from?"

She sighed, then lifted her chin. "No one in Ohio believed it either. But as much as they tried to dig up something on me, there was nothing to find. I'll admit I was completely guilty of being naive. It was easier than asking questions." She exhaled. "I thought that to be a good wife I needed to trust and support my husband in all matters. I learned my lesson. Look, I'm not here to cause any trouble. I promise you won't even know I'm in town."

He doubted that very much. Scanning her face, he tried to figure out the real color of her hair. With her skin tone, she had to be a brunette.

Other than the sleek platinum hairstyle, she looked like a single mom barely making it, no showy jewelry or fancy clothes. Her Mercedes was high-end, but nothing over-the-top. She was a paradox, and he didn't like it.

He knew firsthand that the best con artists didn't look the part. They slipped into a man's life all vulnerable and needy. Like his ex-wife. At their best, no one saw them coming until it was too late. "You just happened on the smallest coastal town in Texas?" Something wasn't adding up, but that was probably his suspicious nature.

"Someone somewhere mentioned it. It sounded like the perfect place to disappear. A place I could rebuild my faith and my life." She laughed. "Yeah, that didn't sound as cheesy in my head."

"There's no family that you can go to?" Hudson asked.

"No family that I can trust or that wants anything to do with me." With a tight smile, she brought her gaze back to his.

She was alone with no one in her corner she could trust. A cold sweat broke out over his body. The desire to offer her help again rammed against his chest. *Good job, Hudson, step right back into that trap you just untangled yourself and your daughter from.*

He had to keep it professional. Refer her to resources that could help her. The women's shelter was just on the other side of the bridge. As he moved to pull out his card to write the information on, Josefina brought Abigail the largest mug of hot chocolate he'd ever seen. Then she sat a plate of warm pumpkin empanadas straight out of the oven onto their table.

Balancing the bottle and holding her daughter with one arm, she twisted to get her wallet out of her diaper bag. "How much?"

"My treat," he said, before she could get into her bag. The silence fell between them again.

"Nope. I've got you both covered." Josefina smiled.

Picking up one of the warm pastries, Hudson grinned at Josefina with total boyish delight. "This is why I will never leave this town."

He slid the plate over to Abigail. "These are the best things I've ever eaten." Now he was avoiding giving her a way out of his town. Wow. He really *did* have a problem.

Biting into the warm pastry, he closed his eyes as the sweet spicy flavor flooded his mouth. So many good textures at one time.

He took another slow bite before he went back to doing his job. "How long do you plan to stay in Port

Del Mar? Do you have a place?" He kept his tone casual. He was asking for professional reasons. He was.

"I'm not sure. The plan was to get here, then figure it out. Maybe find a job?" She was avoiding eye contact again and not eating.

"You traveled thousands of miles without a plan?" Was she serious? The thought of that made his skin itch.

Josefina rubbed her hands together. "You're looking for a place to stay and a job? God must have brought you to our door today!"

"How so?" Abigail asked.

"Well, last weekend, I moved out of the apartment above the *panadería*," the woman explained. "We don't want to rent it to just anyone with it being attached to our shop. And we were just talking about getting some part-time help and maybe offering the apartment as a perk of the job. No early-morning commutes. It's hard to find a place to live here in Port Del Mar—and finding help is just as difficult."

"Really?" Abigail's full lips spread wide and became even more beautiful.

Hudson shook his head. What was Josefina *thinking*? Shouldn't he suggest they perform a background check or something before offering a complete stranger a place to live and a job?

He had heard that the Espinozas' tendency to take in strays was legendary, but this was a bit much. Even for them. "Maybe you should ask each other some questions first. Or at least get some references."

Josefina put her hand on her hip. "Sheriff, you've been stalking her and now interrogating her. Is there a reason I shouldn't rent out the upstairs apartment to her, or give her a job?"

Eyes wide, Abigail stared at him. Pleading. But for what? To keep her secret, or to give the go-ahead to Josefina.

Her moving in above the bakery wouldn't be the worst thing to happen. At least here he could keep an eye on her. Make sure she was on the up-and-up. It was better for his peace of mind to know where she was.

He lifted his hands. "I have nothing negative to say."

With a wide smile, Josefina nodded her head. "Good. I'll show you the apartment, then. It's a small two-bedroom, one bath. It has basic furnishings. Nothing fancy."

"It sounds better than my car."

"Oh, sweetheart." Josefina crossed her hands over her chest. "I'm thankful God merged our paths." She patted Abigail's arm. "It's okay. I've been in your shoes with a baby in my arms, and my family had my back. You're not alone. Let me get the keys, and I think we have a basic lease contract in the filing cabinet. I'll be right back."

The baby arched her back and whimpered.

Concerned, Hudson reached to touch the little forehead. "Is she all right?" Great, now he wanted to take care of her baby.

"I'm not sure. She's usually not fussy, but with all the traveling, maybe she's off. She hasn't had any real floor time to just play. For the last twenty-four hours, she's either been in her carrier or I've been holding her."

The bell rang, and a large group of teens filled the front of the shop. Not a few minutes went by before the door chimed again.

A young woman with three children came in. She smiled at them. "Sheriff." Her gaze moved to Abigail before she hurried the children to the counter. The little shop was filling up. The small crowd were all staring at them with different levels of curiosity.

Abigail leaned closer to him. "Is it just me, or is everyone staring and talking about us? I was getting that at times in Cincinnati, but why here?"

Her daughter let out a cry. She seemed to be done with being held.

Then the poor bell received no breaks for the next five minutes. Abigail sank deeper into her chair as each person came into the bakery. The space became even smaller as people made a point to glance their way. Some were subtle and polite; others not so much.

"Welcome to being the new person in town. And you're talking to the sheriff." He grinned. "All sorts of stories are being spun as we sit here."

"So, if I want to stay under the radar, I should avoid being seen eating with you?"

He didn't like the sound of that, but before he could reply, Josefina returned.

Now she wore a rare frown on her face. "We just got slammed with call-in orders and the counter is busy, so I need to stay and help Margarita. Sheriff, you could show her the apartment. It would give you a chance to interview her and ask any questions you deem important, since you're obviously worried." She laid a ring with two keys on the table between them. With a wink, she turned and went back to the kitchen.

He narrowed his eyes to the retreating Espinoza. The town folk had not been subtle in their attempts to pair him up. They couldn't fathom that a single dad enjoyed being single. It wasn't even lunchtime, and he had a bad feeling that the matchmakers had a new target.

"You don't have to take me up." Abigail went back to bouncing the baby.

Standing, he grabbed the keys. "Your daughter needs a place to rest. You do too."

Abigail turned her baby around, trying a new position. The little one reached for him. He put his hand up, and her chubby fingers wrapped around one of his. "What's her name?"

"Paloma LeRae."

"Hey there, little dove." The biggest eyes blinked up at him. They danced between a gray and a dark green. "She's beautiful. How old is she?"

"You speak Spanish."

"*Sí.*" He grinned at the baby. "My *abuela* was named Paloma. It's a beautiful name."

"Thank you. She's nine months old."

"My daughter just turned six last week."

"You have a daughter?"

He chuckled. "Why do you sound so surprised? I don't look like I'd have kids?"

"Kids?" Her eyes went wide.

"No." He laughed, and people looked. "Just one. Charlotte." He nodded to the back door. "Come on. I'll show you the apartment."

He would open the door for her then leave. There was no reason for him to hang out and spend more time with this woman. The nervous energy he'd picked up from her had to do with the drama she'd left behind in Ohio.

Nothing more.

Which meant there was no need to be personally involved with her to keep an eye out for trouble. If she stayed here at the bakery, she'd be in the middle of town. In plain sight. Word spread like wildfire around here, so if she crossed the line or made a move to take advantage of any one of his people, he'd be here to stop it.

Besides, she probably wouldn't be staying long, anyway. She was used to a much grander lifestyle than a small apartment over a family bakery could offer. He gave her one month, tops, before she became restless and wanted more.

She had a bit too much in common with his ex-wife. At first, they came across as helpless and lost. But it was just an act to get what they wanted. A life of ease and glamor. He was conned once. Not again.

The town would be better off without someone like her.

Who was he kidding? With that smile and baby in her arms, he was the one in danger. But she wouldn't be here long enough to cause true damage. He hoped.

Chapter Three

The diaper bag slipped again, pulling on Abigail's shoulder. She was so tired it was all she could do to keep from falling over herself. Hudson stepped up beside her.

"Let me help." He took the heavy bag and lightened her burden. It felt nice to have someone to lend a hand, but it also scared her. Why was he being so nice? He was married, right?

In her world, men made their own rules and took whatever they wanted. She glanced over at the two women who had defended her and now offered her safety. Without even knowing her.

Their generosity was beyond anything she had ever experienced. Could she trust them? It seemed too easy. Nothing in her life had ever been easy. Not since her mother died, anyway.

In her life, when something seemed too good to be real, it usually was.

"Mrs. Dixon?" Hudson stared at her with his startling eyes.

With an attempt at a smile, she nodded. The air in

her lungs became too heavy, and words were impossible to form. She blinked and cleared her throat. "Please call me Abigail. I think I'm going to drop the Dixon."

"Abigail." His voice offered so much comfort. With his warm hand on her back and her daughter's bag on his shoulder, he guided her up the stairs. She stole a glance at his profile, then quickly forced herself to look ahead.

Maybe God had led her to Port Del Mar because of the Espinoza sisters. If this worked out, it would give her time to find out more about her old family before showing up on their doorstep.

Earlier, the deputy had mentioned the De La Rosa ranch. She had wanted to ask so many questions, but she didn't know how to do that without raising suspicion.

"If you don't want to stay here, I have information about a women's shelter across the bridge."

She stiffened at the top of the stairs. "I don't need a shelter. I can pay for a place to stay." Well, for a couple of months, at least.

Clearing his throat, he opened the door, then moved back to let her in. She didn't move.

He took another step back. "I didn't mean to upset you."

"I'm not upset." That might have been a little sharper than she'd intended. "I'm sure you have better things to do than escort strangers to apartment showings."

The corner of his mouth twitched as if he were fighting a grin. "In a small town like this, the job duties of a sheriff are pretty fluid." He waved to the open door. "Do you want me to stay out here?"

"Oh, no. I'm just..." *Being ridiculous.*

Head up, she walked through the door, then paused.

It was so much more than Josefina had led her to believe. The spacious living room and open kitchen welcomed her. It was perfect.

The neutral walls and floor were a soothing background for the surprises of color in the artwork and pillows that were scattered around. To her right was a clean, modern kitchen, separated from the living room by a farmer's table. The ladder-back chairs were a mix of red, blue and yellow.

The living room was cozy with a light-colored sectional and pillows that matched the chairs. And she was pleased to see there was space on the floor for Paloma and her toys. In the corner was an L-shaped desk with ceiling-to-floor shelves next to it. It had a very delicate, feminine vibe. How did a place she had never even known existed feel so much like home?

"This is nice." He walked in behind her. "It's hard to find long-term rentals in town. If a house is empty, they can make more money renting it to tourists, and there are no apartment complexes. This is a find."

"Do you and your wife have a place in town?"

"Not married. A good friend of mine, the one who encouraged me to run for sheriff, has some properties. I was able to get one with an ocean view."

So, he wasn't married. There was no reason that should be a relief. But it was.

Her daughter squirmed and made a sad crying sound. "Paloma is so tired. I just…" She looked around. What did she want?

Maybe that was what she needed to figure out first. Was this the place?

Wandering around the space, avoiding the intense stare of the sheriff, she ran the tips of her fingers along the edge of the pretty desk. This was too nice. There was no way she could afford this by working part-time at a bakery. To be this close to her dreams and watch them slip away was hard. She couldn't cry, though, not in front of him.

"The bath and bedrooms are down this hall." Hudson's voice startled her out of her thoughts. She nodded and went to investigate, even though this place would never be hers.

The bathroom had a large tub that was begging her to take a long, warm bubble bath, but more importantly would make it easy to bathe Paloma. Across the hall was a small room where a whimsical scene of rabbits playing under the moon was painted in soft colors.

"Josefina is a single mom who has a daughter a couple of years older than mine. This must have been her room. There shouldn't be a problem finding a crib for Paloma."

Tears burned, but she couldn't let them fall. She would have to go to the shelter after all, but this was the place where she wanted to live. The last door was the larger bedroom. It was so much bigger than she was expecting. The soft blue walls and white trim were a perfect setting for the large bed. It was stripped to the mattress, but Abigail could visualize a quilt and throw pillows.

The urge to dive in and cocoon herself pulled at every tired muscle in her body. There was no way she could afford this place. Needing a hand-out made her skin itch, but maybe they would let her crash here tonight. She turned to ask Hudson, but he was gone.

Had he left? Disappointment hit her much harder

than it should have. "Come on, baby girl. I have to tell Josefina that it's a no-go."

Stepping into the living room, she found Hudson leaning on the table, scrolling through his phone.

"Oh, I thought you'd gone." She resented the giddy feeling that bubbled up knowing that he had waited for her.

"Josefina said that you can stay here for now to get some rest. There are sheets in the hallway closet. She'll come up around three to go over the details with you."

He held up his phone. "She didn't have your number, but she wanted you to know that she called her mother." He gave her an apologetic look for some bizarre reason, followed by a tight-lipped smile. "Good news… that means that before the end of the day you will have everything you and Paloma need. And the bad news? If you think the two women downstairs are a force to be reckoned with, wait until you meet their mother. Wonderful woman, but she scares me."

Josefina's mother was coming. Even after all these years, Abigail still missed her mom. Her earliest memories were of her mother calling her Gabby Girl as she cuddled her and they read bedtime stories. Then, without warning, she was gone.

Abigail, or Gabby as they called her at the time, had come home from school and found her oldest brother already there, sitting on the edge of their mother's empty bed. He told her that their mom had gone to heaven. But that didn't make sense—they hadn't finished the story they'd been reading together.

Her mother would have never left without a goodbye kiss. She had always insisted on goodbye kisses every morning.

At nine years old, she couldn't wrap her head around the fact that her mother had vanished. Abigail had been so confused and lost. To this day she didn't understand what happened or what she had done to make her father and brothers so mad that they sent her away without a backward glance.

Just like her mother, they were suddenly out of her life. It had been the first of many lessons in not trusting people who claimed to love you.

She'd barely had time to say a proper goodbye to her mom at the funeral before her great-aunt had ripped her away from her home and family. The woman had hated everything about the De La Rosa family, and she made sure Gabby knew it. Gabby De La Rosa had been erased from existence, and her aunt had dubbed her Gabriella Castillo. It was her mother's maiden name, but it was still as uncomfortable as a pair of secondhand shoes.

"Abigail? Where'd you go?"

"I can't stay here." The air wouldn't circulate through her lungs. Why did it feel like she was losing her family all over again? "I can't imagine I'd be able to make enough working part-time at the bakery for something this nice. I'll have to find something else." Logic had to keep her emotions in check, even though her heart already loved this apartment, the bakery and the sisters.

Why did she get attached to anyone who showed her the simplest kindness? Was there something wrong with her?

Hopefully they would let her stay the night. She'd use the time wisely. Going to the sofa, she pulled out the bottle and tried to feed Paloma again. Her daughter wasn't eating.

"How did you think this was going to play out, when

you arrived in a small town without any connections?" His voice was low and soft, not accusatory or insulting like Brady's when she did something impulsive.

She snorted. "That is a really good question. I was born in Texas, and with everything going on in Ohio, I just had to leave. I trust that God has a plan for me." Now he was going to think she had lost her mind.

"This is ranch country," she said after a long moment. "I always thought I would love working on a ranch. There's housing for the workers, right? I heard Deputy Bridges, their brother, say something about the De La Rosa ranch. Do you know anything about them? Would they be hiring?" There, that sounded logical. She was proud of herself for working her family naturally into the conversation.

"They're a smaller ranch, family-run. They do have cabins they've been known to rent out, but I haven't heard anything about them hiring," he replied. "They tend to hire seasonal day laborers. You'd be better off trying at one of the bigger spreads, like the Wimberly Cattle Company. They have ranch hands and house staff. Several of their employees live on the property." He cleared his throat. "And there are a few other ranches in the area. If you're interested, the Espinoza sisters would be your best connection. They know everyone."

She frowned. That wasn't any help. How could she learn more about her father, brothers and cousins? Maybe the sisters would be more willing to gossip.

Wind rattled the windows. The weather was getting worse. For now, she and Paloma needed a safe warm place to stay.

The idea of asking for charity didn't sit well with her. Voices from the past bombarded her brain. *Use-*

less, undeserving, worthless and *charity case* were just a few of the words. They were lies, she had to remind herself. Not a single one was from God's truth, so she closed her eyes and rebuked them.

"There's still the shelter on the other side of the bridge." His voice brought her back to the room.

Would she be able to get the information she needed if she went there? It wasn't that far, but it felt like a whole different world. She could do that and still work at the bakery, maybe. With her daughter, it was going to be hard to find a normal job.

She wanted to stay here, in Port Del Mar. It was less than a day, but it already felt more like home than any-where else she had ever been. Was it because she was close to her family? They were within her reach, but still so far away.

"I want to find a way to stay in Port Del Mar. I think God brought us here." Her heart tightened. Fighting the urge to ask for his help, she kept her gaze on her daugh-ter. He was not her knight in a cowboy hat.

Hudson stood watching while Abigail spread out a blanket and placed her daughter in the middle. The baby cooed at her mother as she reached for a toy.

Keeping her gaze on the baby, she smiled. "This is what you needed, baby girl."

The image of mother and daughter tugged at his heart. He was intruding on a moment he had no busi-ness being witness to. Tearing his gaze away from the personal interaction, he studied the neat but vibrant apartment. He should leave. She didn't need him here, so there was absolutely no reason for him to stay.

"Something's wrong." She said it more to herself, but

he moved closer. "I wish she could tell me what was going on with her."

Yeah. He wasn't going anywhere. This just became more than a job. He was such an idiot. The last time he tried to play hero to a damsel in distress, she had wrecked him.

He was smarter now. He wouldn't allow that to happen again. The little girl scrunched her face.

Using the back of her hand, Abigail touched the baby's cheeks. "Oh, you're warm. Is this why you've been so fussy?" She finally looked at him. "Could you hand me the backpack? I might have a thermometer in there."

He grabbed the bag off the table and handed it to her.

The little arm started shaking, then the infant went stiff. Her eyes were wide-open, but they didn't have any focus.

"Paloma!" She touched her daughter's face. It didn't look right. "Hudson! Something's wrong."

He rushed to them and kneeled at the side of the tiny body. He gently rolled her to her side. His hands looked so large on the small baby. "Has she had a seizure before?"

"A seizure? No." Abigail's voice was on the edge of panic. "What's happening? She was a little fussy before but fine."

He checked his watch.

"Shouldn't we call 911?" she asked.

"Not yet. We will if it gets closer to four or five minutes."

"*Four minutes?*" She might have screamed that at him. It already seemed like an eternity. Legs tucked under her, Abigail leaned over Paloma and touched her face. "It's okay, baby girl. It's going to be okay. Stay with me. Hudson? It has to be over ten minutes."

There was a pleading in her eyes he hated.

Paloma whimpered as her little body went slack. Abigail breath whooshed out. The seizure had stopped.

"One minute and two seconds." He ran his hand over the baby's forehead. "She feels a little warm, but not too bad." His eyes went to Abigail. "Do you have that thermometer?"

She dug in the backpack, then dumped it in frustration. "It's not here." Dropping the now empty bag, she picked up Paloma and held her close. "I'm so sorry."

Tears dropped on her daughter's cheek and made him feel as useless as snow skis in Texas.

She wiped her face, then her daughter's cheek. "I shouldn't have driven all the way in such a rush."

"It's not your fault. Babies are going to do what they do." He wanted to hold her the way she was holding her daughter. Shifting back, he put more space between them.

"But I drove straight from Cincinnati hardly stopping. She's been in a car for almost twenty hours." The strangled sighs were so sad coming from her. "I'm so sorry. I hate crying. It's a total waste of time."

"You have every right to cry." Hudson stood and held his hand out. "Let's get you off the floor."

Taking her soft hand in his, he lost his breath for a moment. Gritting his teeth against the shock, he shook it off. It wasn't her. Nope. He'd just gone so long without human touch, other than his daughter. He ground his back molars.

She allowed him to help her up, then they both stepped back, away from each other.

"Thank—" another silent sob stole her breath "—you."

"Let me hold her, and you can wash your face." Arms out, he waited for her to respond. "She's safe with me, I promise."

With hesitation, she handed over her daughter. After just staring at the baby in his arms for a few seconds, she finally went to the kitchen sink. He looked down and smiled at the sweet bundle in his arms.

"Your mamma didn't want to let you go." It seemed a lifetime ago when Charlotte was this little. He missed holding her like this. Paloma reached up and grabbed his lip. He leaned in closer and made a popping noise.

At the large white farm sink, Abigail splashed her face. After wiping it dry, she turned and stared at him. "She usually doesn't take to strangers."

"She's a good judge of character." He winked. Then he turned back to Paloma, his expression growing serious. "Knowing that your child is sick and that you can't fix it is the worst feeling in the world." He brought his gaze back to her. "Just a few doors down, there's a women and children's clinic. I think you parked in front of the door. You'll feel better if we get her checked out. I can call over and see if they can fit her in."

She chewed at her bottom lip and glanced to the side, then at her baby. "That would be great. Thank you."

It didn't sound as if accepting help was an easy thing for her to do.

"One warning." He tried to look stern. "Another Espinoza sister is in charge there. Teresa. She's a PA and specializes in women and children's health."

Her eyes went wide. "A cop, two bakers and a PA? How many are there?"

His grin went wide. "There are at least two, maybe three more. Not sure."

"Wow. That's a big family. I thought—" She cut herself off.

"You thought what?" He rocked the baby as her eyelids fluttered.

"Oh nothing. Family. That's a strange concept for me." She pulled down a glass from the cupboard and filled it with tap water.

He had assumed she would be the pure-water-in-a-fancy-bottle type. Would it be safe to stop expecting the worst from her? After taking a long drink, she came back to him. For a minute, she just stared at her daughter in his arms.

Oh no. Was she going to start crying again? "Abigail. It's going to be okay. We'll take her next door and they'll examine her."

With a nod, she held out her hands for her daughter. "Her father has never held her."

There was nothing to say to that, so he gently transferred the baby back to her.

"Oh no! What's that?" she cried out in a broken whisper. "She has blood in her ear." Eyes wide and frantic, she stared at him. "Why would there be blood coming from her ear?"

"Charlotte did that once. It was an ear infection." He got his phone out. "I'll call as we walk to the clinic." Speaker on, he grabbed the bag, then opened the door for Abigail.

So much for keeping his distance.

Chapter Four

Abigail hugged Paloma closer to her chest. Hudson had a gentle hand on her shoulder, guiding her through the door of the clinic. He stayed right next to her as they approached the counter.

The clinic wasn't what she expected. It was warm and inviting. Curved wood inlays in the ceiling were repeated in the desk. Comfortable club chairs were spaced out to look more like a reading nook than a waiting room. Plants were placed in interesting locations.

A woman with silver curls piled on top of her head sat behind the counter. Looking up, she stopped her knitting and smiled at them.

"Sheriff. Resa said you'd be coming in with a sick baby." Her curious gaze darted between Abigail and Hudson.

"Hi, Barb. This is Abigail Dixon and her daughter, Paloma. They just drove in from Ohio."

"Oh my. I drove by myself to Lubbock once to see my son. It was just horrible—and that was only nine hours. I said I'd never do that again. You must be worn-out…and the poor little one is sick." She lifted a clipboard with a pen tied to it. "You'll need to fill these forms out, but you can do it in the room."

Abigail shifted, intending to move Paloma to one arm so she could take the paperwork, but Hudson stepped forward and took it.

"Let me help. You have your arms full, and I'm sure you don't want to disrupt her."

Barb's perfectly shaped brow arched with unspoken questions. "Well, then, you can both come this way." She was all business as she escorted them down the hall. Except for the slight smirk. Abigail couldn't even imagine what that meant.

"The PA will be in to see you shortly." Barb closed the door behind her.

The exam room had an oversize watercolor painting of wildflowers on one wall. Posters illustrating the development of a baby's first year covered another.

Three miniature rosebushes grew in the bay window. In the corner was a cozy rocking chair. A neat stack of children's books and gardening magazines sat on a vintage side table. Next to the exam table was a wicker basket full of toys.

She and Paloma were alone with Hudson in a very small room. Not knowing what to do, Abigail just stood there. Her heart rate accelerated, and her skin felt too warm. She hadn't been this uncomfortable with him before.

With a nod of his chin, Hudson motioned to the rocking chair. "Sit. Relax. She'll be here soon. I'll help fill out the paperwork while you hold Paloma, then I'll leave."

She looked at the paperwork in his hands. In bold letters at the top, it asked: Name.

"Thank you." Averting her eyes, she sat in the rocker and forced her attention to Paloma. Her daughter's thick lashes lay against her soft cheeks.

Name. That should be a straightforward question. Everyone knew their own name, but she'd had three names in her life. The one she was born with, Gabby De La Rosa. The one her aunt gave her after her mother died, Gabriella Castillo, and the one her husband gave her, Abigail Dixon. None of them really felt like her, but at the same time they were all a piece of her.

She wasn't ready to deal with the family she didn't know, but she didn't want to be a Dixon anymore either. There needed to be as much distance between them and her ex-husband as possible.

"First one is easy. Name." He printed Paloma's name, then hers. "Abigail is short for anything?"

There was nothing easy about her name. She looked to the ceiling in a futile attempt to find answers.

"Abigail?"

She didn't have the time or energy to explain her whole messed-up life. "Gabriella. But I haven't used that in years."

"Next question. Phone number."

She pulled her cell out of her pocket. "It's new. I haven't memorized it yet."

He filled in her number. "Okay. Work phone. Not yet." He put a slash through it.

She sighed. Did she even count as a full person?

He pulled his mouth to the side, then looked at her. Sympathy shadowed his piercing gaze. "Home address?"

Her lungs tightened, and the ice that had been in her lungs now burned her throat. She didn't have a home address. What was she doing here in Texas? Her daughter was sick and needed stability. She had no idea how she was going to make this work.

Coming to Port Del Mar had only made things worse. She had failed her daughter. They were homeless.

"Abigail?" He had the voice of a professional talking someone off the ledge.

Blinking, she made sure her eyes were dry before she looked up at him, but then quickly dropped her gaze. "I don't have an address. Can we skip it?"

His jaw went hard. "Abigail. Look at me."

She did, and the blue one looked deeper as the gold iris burned. It took all the strength she had, but she managed to move her gaze to the roses in the window. Such a warm, homey touch. An image of her mother trimming a climbing rosebush filled her thoughts. Was it still there? Had someone taken care of it, or had they just let it die? Her mother had loved that rosebush.

"Abigail, you can put the apartment above the bakery, or there's the shelter across the bridge. I could call and see if they have room tonight."

She shook her head. "I want to stay close, so I guess for today it's the apartment. I hope I can stay the night at least." The rosebush didn't matter now. All of her attention went to the tiny person sleeping in her arms. It was her responsibility to make sure Paloma never felt lost and alone. "I don't know if I can afford it or what they're asking for the deposit."

"I'm sure they'll work something out until you're on your feet. Her birthday?"

"She was born on July 25." That one was easy. She took a deep breath.

"Next of kin?" Her eyes went wide, and when she

jerked her face up to look at him, she found his gaze was on her. Concern, or maybe pity, filled those mesmerizing eyes.

And, just like that, it got worse. They wanted an emergency contact. Next of kin. All she had was a family that didn't want her. They didn't even know she was in town. She dropped her head and closed her eyes.

"I…um." Abigail's throat threatened to close. Her aunt was glad she was gone. Would her father even acknowledge her? Two brothers and cousins she grew up with had turned their backs on her. There wasn't anyone. "I don't think an ex-husband in prison counts, does it?"

Leaning on the exam table, Hudson sat the clipboard down. "Abigail."

"No. Leave it blank. I don't have anyone I would call or who would want to hear from me." A year ago, she hadn't thought life could get worse. And now here she sat with a sick child, relying on complete strangers. Yeah, she had been so wrong.

Lifting her chin, she dared him to feel sorry for her. She was a survivor. God had gotten her through darker days, and he would get her through this as well. If only she could make better choices.

There was no shift in his expression. As a lawman, he'd probably heard all sorts of sad tales. Silence stretched between them as they studied each other.

He spoke first. With a curt nod he picked up the paperwork. "I'll put myself down for now. You might also ask the Espinoza sisters. They're good people. You can trust them."

They might be wonderful people, but she didn't see herself trusting anyone. She just wanted to be strong enough to stand on her own and be independent. The only problem was that she had no idea how to make that happen.

"Insurance?" His voice hesitated for the first time. "Do you have medical insurance?" He cleared his throat. "The clinic will work with you if you don't."

"I do." She sighed. For the next few months, anyway. She hated being a charity case, but what else could she do for now? Anger burned in her gut at everything they had lost because of Brady's greed.

Why? So he could have an even bigger house, fancier cars and wear only shoes with red soles. It was all to impress people that didn't matter.

She had never wanted any of that.

Her dreams had been of a cozy house with a little backyard and a park within walking distance. She wanted mornings and evenings at a family table filled with love. Building a family, not an empire, had been her dream.

"Abigail?"

"Sorry. It's in the bag."

"Let me take her, and you can get your card." Hudson lowered the diaper bag off his shoulder, then one big arm slipped under hers to lift Paloma up against his chest. Her daughter snuggled into his shirt and made sweet cooing noises. She was so tiny.

Before they went any farther down the list, a soft knock brought Abigail's head up. The door opened, and a woman obviously related to the Espinoza sisters peeked in with a huge smile.

Her shoulder-length hair was pulled back, and dark curls fell around her neck. "Hello. I'm PA Espinoza. Please call me Resa." She stepped into the room and gently closed the door behind her. "Oh, hello, Sheriff. I wasn't expecting you to be in here."

"Just assisting with the paperwork."

"He was helping with the questions. Or trying to, anyway. I haven't finished. There are some… I'm not sure—" She wasn't going to cry in front of this woman.

Taking the clipboard and placing it on top of the magazines, the PA gently patted Abigail's arm. The compassion on the woman's face had Abigail on the edge of tears again.

"It's okay. Being in a new place with a sick baby is very stressful. We'll fill out the forms together after I take a look at her."

Resa was taller than her sisters but had the same dark hair and eyes. Eyes filled with compassion, the same as those of the other two women. All her focus was on Paloma as she took her temperature. "It's 99.7. A little elevated but not bad. You two have quite the fan club. I hear you had an adventure on your first day in town."

"She's never been sick before. I shouldn't have taken her on a long road trip. I only stopped a couple of times."

"Place her on the table, and we'll have a look at this precious little girl." She patted the table, and Hudson gently eased her down on top of the strip of paper. Paloma opened her eyes and looked up at him with a smile. She reached for his lip before he could get far enough away. With a chuckle, he pried her fingers away.

Abigail stood next to him and stroked her baby's hair. "She's never sick."

"She's got a healthy grip." The PA smiled at them, then moved to examine her. "On the phone, Hudson said she'd never had a seizure before? But you've been traveling?"

"That's correct." She glanced at him. His attention was fully on her daughter. He must be a good father. She wasn't sure she even believed there was such a thing. "Is it too cold and windy for her to be out? I drove in from Ohio. I didn't even know she had a fever. She never seemed hot or uncomfortable until I was in the bakery. Was it the long trip?"

"No, I don't think so."

"What caused the seizure?"

"Since this is her first, it will be hard to say what brought it on. She might not ever have another. But if she does, we can look at common factors. It looks as if she has an ear infection."

"Is that bad?"

Hudson's eyes lifted to hers. "Charlotte had them when she was little. She outgrew them." His voice was reassuring.

Resa nodded. "The ear infection will be easy to treat. We just have to stay on top of it. Since she didn't run a fever, you'll have to look for other clues that she isn't feeling well. If they become chronic then we'll discuss other treatments."

"Treatments? If she doesn't have a fever, how will I know she's sick?" Abigail listened to every suggestion and stamped it on her brain. She'd make a list as soon as she could. "I felt so helpless."

Resa laid a hand over hers. "First rule. Kids get sick. You can't blame yourself. Two. Take a deep breath and relax. Babies are very resilient. Plus, you have Margarita and Josefina. My sisters will be mothering you until you want to go into hiding."

"What do I do now?"

"I'm going to give you some medication to start today. The pediatrician is at the clinic on Wednesdays."

"What if something happens before then? That's two days away." Hudson was frowning at the woman as if she had insulted them.

She smiled. "If they need anything, I'm only a call away. They can always find me." She scooped up Paloma and handed her to Abigail. "Go ahead and relax in the rocking chair and we'll finish the paperwork. It's mostly medical history and release forms."

Once Abigail was settled in the rocking chair, Resa pulled up a round stool with wheels and sat in front of them, clipboard in hand.

Hudson moved to the door, then stood awkwardly for a minute. "You've got this. I'm going to head out now. But you have my number, so don't hesitate to call."

"Thank you so much for your help. I don't know what I would have done if I'd been alone."

"You would have been fine, but I'm glad I was there to lend a hand. See you at the bakery." He left, gently closing the door behind him.

There was no rational reason for her to feel so alone at the click of the doorknob.

Resa touched her arm, then winked. "Now, having the sheriff as your personal escort is a pretty nice small-town service. He's a good man, but a smidge closed off as far as personal relationships go."

Abigail wasn't sure how she was supposed to respond to that. Was she being warned off? The thought was funny. Should she tell the woman she was completely closed off to any sort of relationship too?

Flipping to the second page of the paperwork, Resa asked her a few health questions. Then she put it aside and gave her another gentle smile. "You know, the mammas of this town have been trying to set him up since the day he arrived." She twisted her mouth to the side. "They might have met their match in that one. He's proven stronger than their collective power."

It took a minute for Abigail to catch up. "I'm sure Sheriff Menchaca will do whatever he thinks is right. From the moment I came into town, everyone's been over-the-top nice. It's kind of scary. Am I in one of those psychological thriller movies where nothing is what it seems to be? I'm waiting for the monster to appear and wondering how I'm going to save my daughter. Should I run now, or is it already too late?"

Resa laughed. "Oh, it's too late. Welcome to Port Del Mar. Where the danger of being smothered by love and kindness is very real."

"Everyone has been so helpful. I just want to make sure I don't do anything to make Paloma worse. I've already dragged her across the country. How am I going to make sure she stays healthy?"

"Well, first of all, you are going to get some rest. And if you need help, you will ask for it." She winked as she handed her a white paper sack. "We have some samples of antibiotics and Tylenol that you can use."

"It's safe for a baby? She has never been sick before."

"It's made for infants. I'll give you directions to follow. If you have any questions or concerns, call me. Better yet, tell my sisters. They always manage to get a hold of me." She smiled. "I know it's scary. But you're not alone."

"Thank you so much." Abigail pressed her lips together and stood, gently shifting Paloma to her shoulder.

"My sisters can be a bit overzealous when it comes

to taking care of people, but they are an incredible resource. Once you become their mission, nothing is going to stop them from taking care of you."

"But I don't want to be someone's mission. I just want to stand on my own."

"I totally get that. But sometimes we need support to get there. It's okay to get some help to build up to those first steps after we've been knocked down."

Abigail's head was swimming. How had these people just entered her life? If they were all on the up-and-up, it had to be a God thing. Could she trust them? More to the point, could she afford *not* to trust them?

The PA stood. "Okay, we're done here for now. Go get some rest. You need it as much as your girl does."

Resa went down on her haunches in front of her so that she could make eye contact. "Should I call someone to walk you back? I could check to see if Sheriff Menchaca is still out front."

She stood. "No. No. I'm good. It's just been an incredibly long couple of days that don't seem to have an end, and my brain is fried. Getting to the apartment and taking a nap sounds like the perfect remedy. Thank you for everything."

Resa opened the door. "*De nada*. It's my pleasure. Let Barb know you'll be coming on Wednesday."

Abigail stopped by the front counter to schedule a follow-up appointment, then stepped outside. For a second, her sight blurred and there was an odd floating sensation in her head.

Sheriff Hudson Menchaca was standing not far from the door. But he wasn't alone. A pretty brunette was nodding at whatever he was telling her.

He glanced over the woman's shoulder, and they

made eye contact. He instantly smiled, then frowned. His forehead creased.

The woman turned to see what had grabbed his attention. She smiled too. Both of them walked toward her.

Out of habit, Abigail pulled back slightly, then stopped herself and stood straighter. Her head did the weird, swimming, upside-down thing.

"Abigail, this is our mayor, Selena De La Rosa. She—"

Abigail didn't hear another word. Her oldest brother, Xavier, had had a girlfriend named Selena. Was this the same one? He had given the girl their pet dog.

No one had even asked her. One morning he just took Luna for a walk and came back without her. The reason? Selena had needed the dog more than they did.

But that wasn't true. She had loved that dog, and she had decided she didn't like his girlfriend. Tears welled up at the memory.

She blinked and tried to focus. It was so long ago, not now. Shadowed worms darted across her vision. She couldn't clear her thoughts. This was someone who might be a part of her family.

"Abigail?" Hudson's strong voice cut through the fog.

She wanted to ask so many questions, but she wasn't ready for this.

He was next to her. His arms protecting Paloma. She wasn't able to utter one word. The world turned upside down and then went dark.

Chapter Five

Abigail's lids didn't want to open. It was as if someone had glued them shut. Squeezing, she tried again. *Paloma!* Where was her daughter? Ripping her lids apart, she shot up. Attempted to, anyway, but there was something in her way.

Her eyes finally cooperated. Not that it helped. It was too dark to see anything. Where was she? Her fingers dug into the soft, pillowy covering of the bed where she was cocooned.

As her sight adjusted, she took in the feminine room. There was an IV in her arm. Was she in the clinic?

Her heart rate jacked up, she twisted around, searching for her daughter.

Paloma was in a crib next to the bed. Ella's pulse finally settled. Blinking, she tried to clear her head. Port Del Mar. She was in the apartment above the bakery.

She glanced at the IV bag. What had happened and why was she here instead of the clinic?

There was no sunlight shining through the curtained window. How long had she been asleep?

Falling back, she groaned and closed her eyes. It all

came back. She must've fainted in front of him and the woman who might be married to her brother. Selena De La Rosa. Right in the middle of Main Street. Could this be any more embarrassing? So much for lying low and not drawing any attention.

She glanced at the needle in her arm. It couldn't be too bad if they'd brought her to the apartment, right?

Sitting up, she swung her feet to the side of the bed where Paloma lay sleeping. Had Hudson brought her to the apartment? Carried her up the steps? Was he still here?

Deep breath. *Okay, God. We are in Port Del Mar. What happens now?*

She had come here on faith alone. She needed to keep her focus on Him and let her faith guide her. Obviously, there was no way she could do this alone right now. She had collapsed. God had brought her here. She needed to trust Him. There was no person that would take care of her like her God would.

Standing on weak legs, she made it to her daughter. Paloma had flipped onto her back with her arms above her head and her face turned to the side. Her baby girl looked so tranquil as she slept, not a care in the world. She had no clue how precarious their situation was. As her mother, it was Abigail's job to keep it that way as long as possible.

Paloma was going to be raised by a strong woman who relied on God and no one else. If her father and the rest of the family turned out to be as bad as her aunt said, then she would move on.

"Hola." A voice from behind Abigail startled her. Turning she found an older woman with a thick silver braid and the warmest smile. She stood and crossed the room. "I'm Maria Espinoza. Go get back in bed. If you need to hold your daughter, I'll bring her to you. No more falling."

"You're Mrs. Espinoza. Their mother?" This tiny woman was the one everyone had warned her was bossier than Margarita and Josefina?

The older woman laughed with a beauty that took Abigail's breath. The woman was mesmerizing, radiating pure joy. "*Sí*. That would be me. Did they tell you to run? My children have no respect for me." The wide smile said she didn't believe what she'd just said. "Do you want your baby? To be safe, you should sit while holding her. I can bring her to you."

Reluctant to go back to the bed but still feeling lightheaded, Abigail did as she was told. "No. She needs her sleep. She looks so peaceful. Why am I here?"

"My daughters agreed with me this would be a better place for us to care for you than in the clinic. Your baby is feeling much better. She took a full bottle and ate some squash from my garden. Josefina steamed and pureed it. With her tummy full and the medicine Resa gave you, she is on the road to being strong and healthy. I had an extra crib no one was using, and the sheriff was kind enough to set it up. That was very nice of him, *sí*?"

"Yes. He's been very kind. So has your family." She looked up at the line attached to her arm. "Why the IV bag?"

"You were dehydrated. It was a blessing for you to fall in front of the clinic and that Sheriff Menchaca was there to help. When was the last time you ate?"

She frowned. It hadn't been that long, had it? "I don't know. Maybe an empanada." Had she eaten it?

Tsking, Maria came over to the bed and fluffed Abigail's pillows. "Everyone is very worried about you. Let me bring you some *caldo*. It's on the stove. Soup is good when you haven't eaten in a while."

"I'll go with you and sit at the table. This bed is too beautiful to eat on." She removed the needle from her arm. The bag was almost empty, anyway.

"Let me help you." The mother of all the Espinoza siblings —and seemingly the heart of the community— put her arm around Abigail's waist. The woman barely reached her shoulder, but Abigail had no doubt she was strong enough to get them both to where they were going.

When they entered the living area, Josefina and Margarita turned to them with smiles. "You look rested. Now you're ready to eat."

Settled at the table, Abigail felt her stomach rumble. The aroma coming from the stove was mouthwatering.

Maria set a glass of water in front of her. "Drink."

She drank. A large bowl of the savory soup sat on the table, next to a stack of tortillas. Before Abigail could dig in, the door opened.

The sheriff, who had seen her at her worst, stepped into the room. He carried several bags the color of a bright sunny day. Each was overflowing with groceries. He froze when he saw her.

"Uh… Sorry, I should have knocked."

"Ya, ya." Maria waved her hand in the air. "Come in. Put this here. Oh, you've brought your special helper with you."

A little girl of about six came up behind him with two small bags. "Hi, Ms. E. Look how strong I am." She lifted the canvas tote. With a show of being very impressed, Maria took the bags from her.

"Hi. I'm Charlotte. My dad is the sheriff, and he let me help bring these bags of food in for you. Are you the lady that fainted?"

With a big yellow bow in her dark hair the little girl's smile radiated from her eyes. Standing, Abigail went to help, but Maria waved her off.

"Hello, Charlotte. And yes, unfortunately, I am the lady that fainted."

"Her name is Mrs. Dixon," Hudson gently told his daughter.

"Oh no. Please call me Abigail. I'm just Abigail."

"Where's your baby?" The little girl was now whispering. "I love babies, but Daddy told me I had to be quiet because she doesn't feel good."

"Charlotte, they're tired and don't need visitors." Josefina and Margarita were emptying the bags Hudson had put on the counter. "We are about to leave ourselves."

Eggs, milk, bread and a wide variety of fresh vegetables kept coming out of the totes. "Oh, I can't take all this food."

"Nonsense." Maria waved her off. "You are helping me too. My garden is too big and my chickens are too happy. I have more than I could possibly use. So, *thank you*." She turned to the man that towered over her. "Sheriff, have you eaten?"

"Yes," Hudson mumbled, but his daughter contradicted him.

"No. We had a snack, but he said we'd pick up something on the way home." She stood on her toes to look up at the stove and sniffed. "That smells so good."

Abigail bit back a laugh as Hudson closed his eyes and sighed.

"We really should go." He glanced at her, then back to Maria.

The older woman shook her head. "Stay. We are scheduled to help organize and distribute supplies for the food bank tonight. It would be great if you were here to eat with her." She leaned closer to him. "I would worry a lot less if I knew you were here for a bit. Just long enough for everyone to eat."

Maria straightened and smiled at Abigail as if no one else had heard what she'd told the sheriff. "So, sit. I'll make you and Charlotte a bowl before we leave."

Hudson's eyes shifted to Abigail. "I um… I still have the playpen to bring up."

Maria shooed him away toward the table. "You can get that after you eat." She gestured to his daughter while making her way to the stove. "Charlotte, will you take the bowls to the table, please?"

"Yes, ma'am." The child bounced as she held her hands out. "Thank you. You make the best dinners." Guilt clouded her eyes as she turned to her dad with the first bowl. "You make good dinners too, Daddy. But Ms. Maria's have something extra."

Abigail spoke without filtering her thoughts. "It's a mother's love. It's the best ingredient." After the words were out, she lowered her head in embarrassment. She had just insulted him. Great.

"I don't think my mother ever made me dinner." Charlotte's gaze went to the ceiling as if she were trying to remember, but she didn't seem sad. "Did she, Daddy?"

"No. She didn't." With three bowls on the table, Charlotte scooted a chair in close to him. "Well, you make the best macaroni and cheese and grilled cheese.

That's my favorite. And broccoli with cheese." She looked at Abigail, her bright eyes full of pure joy and innocence. "I love cheese, and Daddy does all those the best." Her eyes went wide and she wiggled in her chair.

"Daddy, I need to—" her eyes darted around the room "—I need to visit the little girls' room."

He pointed the way to the hall. "Don't forget to wash your hands. If you need help, let me know."

"I'm a big girl. I know how to wash my hands. Germs are bad."

Maria added a freshly heated tortilla to the basket on the table. "Sheriff, you are not sitting yet." She was not taking no for an answer. Apparently, there were no limits to who was bossed around.

Abigail smiled at him and pointed to the empty chair. "Might as well join me. She's not letting you leave without eating."

"Smart woman." Turning off the stovetop, Maria took off the apron she was wearing. "Come on, girls, it's time for us to leave."

"My mother doesn't offer to leave people alone very often. Better take advantage and run." Josefina put up the last of the dishes she had been washing and picked up her purse. "I'm kidding about my mother. Sort of."

"No, she's not." Margarita's mouth was in a flat line. "My mother believes it's her responsibility to take care of everyone that enters her realm."

"Then I guess y'all come by it honestly," Abigail blurted out. Hudson laughed.

"What? *Us?*" the sisters said at the same time, then groaned.

"I hate it when we do that." Josefina glared at her older sister, who just laughed. "Really, you might need to be very stern with her. She drove our older brother to Oklahoma to get away from her mothering."

Maria glared at her daughters. "He came back."

"Because he was shot!" Margarita sighed and tossed a bag over her shoulder.

"Oh no. Is he okay?" Abigail asked.

"He's fine now." Josefina was by the door now. "You met him. He's one of the sheriff's deputies. But really, our mother doesn't know when to stop."

Margarita continued the story without missing a beat. "He ended up moving out of the house and into the middle of the De La Rosa ranch with three gates to keep her out." A spark of mischief in her eyes, she hugged her mother. "We'll be downstairs loading the boxes. Mother, if you're not down in ten minutes, we will leave without you." They went out the door.

"My daughters always threaten, but they never follow through. I'm sorry if I get a little overbearing. I just need to make sure everyone is safe."

"It's okay. It's been a long time since anyone has mothered me. I appreciate it." Abigail tucked her head and stared at the food in front of her. Why had she said that? Her mouth was running all over the road without any attention to warning signs.

Which meant that she was already too comfortable with these wonderful people and was not guarding her emotions. Not good.

The chair next to her scraped the floor, and the older woman's warm hand reached for hers.

"Oh, *mija*, I'm so sorry. How old were you when you lost your mother?"

Should she lie? Change the subject? But she couldn't.

Her mother had loved her so much, and no one ever really wanted to hear about her. "Nine."

Maria's fingers briefly tightened around her hand. "My children lost their father at such a young age, too. That kind of tragedy shapes a person. Do you have brothers or sisters? Was your father there for you?"

Not knowing what to say, she looked out the window. "There wasn't anyone. I went to live with an older aunt."

"Oh, *mija*. I'm sorry. I don't know what I would have done without my family. This must be why God brought you to us." Her other hand came up, and she lowered her voice. "That also must be why you and the sheriff have connected so quickly. He understands loss and tragedy too. He grew up without his mother. A senseless shooting." She gripped Abigail's arm and then Hudson's, tears in her eyes. "But you both have us now. And you have God." Standing, she wiped her face. Her voice was so strong and filled with confidence. Abigail really wanted to believe her.

Hudson stiffened and looked away. He didn't say anything, but he didn't look happy about his own life being talked about. How old had he been when he'd lost his mom?

"Thank you," Abigail managed to whisper. "Your kindness means so much to me."

Maria stood. "Okay, time for me to go. Thank you for staying, Sheriff. It eases my nervous heart."

"I don't believe there is anything nervous about you, Mrs. Espinoza. But thank you for this excellent dinner. I'll make sure everything is secure before we leave for the night."

Abigail said goodbye to Maria as well but couldn't take her gaze off the man sitting across from her. He had become stiff, looking at everything but her. He was not happy at being forced to have dinner with her or was it the mention of his mother?

Charlotte bounced into the room and scooted into her chair. "I heard the baby moving around."

"Charlotte Menchaca, did you really?" Hudson lowered his chin, then he looked at Abigail for the first time since they had talked about their mothers. "She will do just about anything to be around babies. She is a little obsessed."

"No, Daddy. I promise. I came right back here." She turned her big eyes to Abigail. "Will you go get her? I do love babies. I want a little sister—or even a brother—but Daddy says I can't have everything I want."

"Give us all a chance to finish our dinner." He handed his daughter a tortilla, then offered Abigail one before taking a second one for himself. "We'll check on the baby when we're done. She isn't fussing."

"Maybe I should go check on her." Abigail looked to the hallway. He was right that Paloma wasn't crying out for her, but what if something was wrong?

Hudson grunted—or maybe it was a chuckle. Was he laughing at her? She stopped the backward motion of the chair. "What?"

"Maria was right. You need a keeper."

That caused her spine to stiffen. "I do not." She kept her voice low and steady. Sheriff Menchaca would *not* get a rise out of her.

With a glint in his eyes, he leaned over his bowl. The left corner of his mouth quirked up. "You haven't taken two bites of your dinner and you're all ready to run. That baby is sound asleep." He eased back and tore off a piece of his tortilla. "This is the best *caldo* you are ever going to eat. Sit back and enjoy. You can't take care of Paloma if you're too weak to pick her up. We'll get your baby girl as soon as the bowl is empty."

Her skin heated. She was probably turning red. What she hated the most was that he was right. Closing her eyes, she said a little prayer for her pride to take a back seat. When she opened them, she kept her focus on the warm soup in front of her and gave thanks.

Charlotte was chatting about her day in school and asking Abigail a ton of questions about Paloma and why she came to Port Del Mar. Abigail wasn't able to keep track of the rapid-fire questions, but she enjoyed the little girl's chatter.

"How much longer will Paloma sleep? I love babies, but since I don't have a mom, Daddy says I can't have a little brother or sister." Her words were a little muffled since she also had food in her mouth. "Either would be nice, but I think a sister would be nicer. Does Paloma have a dad?"

"Charlotte." Hudson's voice was the epitome of patience. "You can't eat and talk at the same time. And Mrs. Dixon can't eat if she is answering your questions."

"Oh! And Mrs. E. said you need to eat." With a big sigh, his daughter smiled at her, then tore off a chunk of tortilla and scooped up a piece of meat, just like her dad was doing.

Did her father eat dinner with the family? She remembered helping her mom and cousin Belle in the kitchen, but it was fuzzy. Closing her eyes, she thought of the family table, but she imagined them all grown-up. Her father would hug her, thrilled she had finally returned. He would explain how they had tried to get her back, but her aunt blocked them.

She relaxed back in her chair. They would be so happy to have her home, and she would help them make dinner. They would ask her about her life and tell her everything she had missed.

But her aunt had made sure she knew that was all just wishful thinking. Her family didn't want her. Only her mother had loved her, and she was gone.

"Abigail?" The concerned voice was low and soothing.

Blinking, she opened her lids and found Hudson and Charlotte staring at her. Smiling, she shook her head. "Sorry. Got lost in my thoughts." Thoughts that would not help her build a new life. She lifted her spoon and made a show of eating.

"I have a joke," Charlotte announced. "Knock, knock."

Hudson gave her a side-eye, but his mouth was quirked at the corner. "Who's there?"

"Booooo," she whispered.

He leaned closer. "Boo, who?"

Her small hand reached up and touched his cheek. "Don't cry. I'm here to help."

Chuckling, he leaned back, pretending he had never heard the joke before. "That's funny. Now eat or I'll cry for real."

Abigail sighed. This was what it was like to have a family. To sit at the table after a long day and enjoy each other's company. To tell silly jokes and smile. To hear about the events and people that passed through their lives. But this wasn't real either. The sheriff had been coerced into having dinner with her.

Wishes and dreams of family dinners had no place in reality—and the real world was where she had to raise her daughter.

Chapter Six

Hudson narrowed his eyes to force his attention on Mayor De La Rosa's words. His mind kept wanting to stare at the clinic door. Abigail had been in Port Del Mar for three days, and now she and Paloma were seeing the doctor.

He had made a conscious effort to stay away after they'd had dinner together at Maria's. To be fair, it had been an intense day—but still, he should not be this preoccupied with her. It was like his brain had reverted to junior high and all he could think about was the girl who had caught his fancy.

He was too old and experienced not to have better control of his thoughts.

"Sheriff Menchaca?" Selena De La Rosa, the mayor of this sleepy little town, tilted her head to gain eye contact. "Is there something going on at the clinic I should know about? You're very distracted."

With a forced smile, he shook his head. But before he could ask her to repeat her question, the door opened.

Abigail was in a long red coat, the sharp line of her blond hair peeking out from under a black beanie. She covered Paloma in the blanket before stepping out onto the sidewalk. His lame heart twisted in a strange joy.

No, he wasn't happy to see her. It was his job to make sure she didn't bring trouble into his territory. The people of Port Del Mar had elected him to protect them after all.

Her history and reasons for being here were shady at best. He didn't like unsolved puzzles. That was it. She was a riddle that needed an answer. An answer he believed.

She scanned the street, and then her gaze found his. He was on the sidewalk between her and the bakery. Her chin darted down, and she adjusted the blanket around Paloma.

Why was she just standing here? His inspection of her didn't go unnoticed. For a moment, she lifted her head and stared back at him. Her shoulders rose as she took a deep breath, then, with a straightened spine, she walked forward. The word *magnificent* echoed through his head. He bit down hard on his back molars.

"Oh, I see. There were rumors that you were taken with our new visitor and her baby. It's good to see her out and about. She looks better than she did the other day." The mayor turned to him and studied his face with a smirk. "I didn't believe it. But I've seen it with my own eyes. You're smitten."

"No. Her daughter had a seizure the first day." He shrugged and made sure to look at the mayor. "Abigail had pushed herself too far. But there are also some issues with her past, and I don't like what that could mean for our citizens. For the most part, they are hardworking, honest people, and I don't want anyone taking advantage of them."

Selena's mouth pressed into a hard line, obviously suppressing another laugh. Her gaze cut to the woman and child he was working hard to ignore. "Yes," she said with sarcastic sternness, "I can see the threat she poses."

"The most damage is done when people let down their guard, trusting that they're safe."

She leaned closer, her eyes wide. "Tell me more about the horrible mayhem this single mom and baby can wreak on our town."

Shoving his hands in his pockets, he resisted the urge to defend himself again. "I thought you were worried about the bored teens causing havoc in the area. We should go back to the station and talk with a few of the local deputies, get some ideas."

Selena pulled her lips between her teeth, obviously trying to suppress laughter at his expense. She nodded. "I agree this is important. But we should schedule a meeting and get all the right parties involved. Maybe your time would be better spent investigating the atrocities Mrs. Dixon and her little baby could bring down on the innocent people of Port Del Mar? To protect us all, you could escort her to the apartment above the bakery. As a bonus, bring back some of those pumpkin empanadas. Then we'll talk." The sly smile was emboldened with a wink. From the mayor.

She had never given him that particular expression before. He rolled his eyes to the sky. Not her too.

Turning to the woman who had been lurking in his mind without permission, he noticed that Abigail looked stronger but still stressed. Was something still wrong with Paloma?

Selena was talking. It was probably something he should be listening to, but he couldn't keep his gaze from Abigail and Paloma. Did the baby have another seizure? There was a good chance Abigail wasn't getting enough sleep or food. Was she eating?

To derail his chaotic thoughts, he turned to stare at the ocean waves. They were high today. The wind was chilly as it came off the water. The cold stung his skin.

Selena stepped forward as Abigail approached, her hand out. "Hello. I would love to give you another welcome to Port Del Mar. I hope you are both feeling better."

His good manners forced him to stop staring at the ocean and greet Abigail. "Hi. It's good to see you. Abigail, you met the mayor of our sleepy beach town the first day you were here. Mayor Selena De La Rosa, this is Abigail and Paloma Dixson. Fresh from Cincinnati."

Abigail's smile became forced. "Mayor De la Rosa?"

"No, just Selena. Our town is way too small for the title of mayor to really mean anything. I basically just get to do all the stuff no one else wants to do. Our sheriff here is the real deal. He keeps the town moving along without any troubles."

Abigail's gaze darted between them. "I wasn't expecting to see you outside the clinic today." She bit the corner of her mouth and looked away, as if regretting her words.

"I saw Mayor De La Rosa here and needed to update her on some issues. I forgot today was Paloma's follow-up appointment at the clinic." *Okay, that was bad.* He had never been a liar. He hated liars. His head was all messed up, and over a woman. He knew better.

Abigail blinked and stared at Selena. "De La Rosa? Like the ranch?"

"Ye-es." Hesitation stretched the word into two syllables. "It's officially called the Diamondback Ranch. You've heard of it? It's a small operation."

Pulling her baby closer, Abigail fussed with the blanket, not making any eye contact. "On the first day, someone mentioned it."

Now she was looking extremely uncomfortable. Out of an instinct to protect, Hudson stepped closer. "Yeah. Bridges came into the bakery and was talking about some kids causing problems. Probably the same ones that vandalized the dock. Abigail had asked about working on a ranch."

Nodding, she kept her gaze focused on her baby. "I thought that would be fun, and I'd heard that people lived on the ranch where they worked. I needed a place to live." She pulled her bottom lip between her teeth, then looked up at Selena. "Is it your ranch? Do you live there?"

"No. My husband's family owns the ranch. He's the oldest, but we live in town. His cousin and he run several of the local businesses. Are you still looking for work? He would be able to hook you up. But rumor has it that you're working for the Espinozas' bakery. Or will be soon."

"Yes. They've been great." Her bright eyes now stared at the mayor with a new intensity. "So, his father runs the ranch? Are there many siblings and cousins? Working with family must be nice."

Hudson narrowed his eyes. What was she up to? Earlier she had asked about working on the Diamondback Ranch, now she wanted to know the family tree? "You still looking for work on a ranch? I thought you were going to take the job at the bakery and live in the apartment above the shop. Is that not working out?" He crossed his arms and leaned back on his monster Jeep.

"I, uh—"

Selena gave him a side-eye, then smiled at Abigail. "If you're still looking for work on a ranch, you can talk to Belle. She is my husband's cousin and pretty much runs the daily operations out there. But Xavier—that's my husband—does have a restaurant and a gift shop on the pier. He and his cousin have a fleet of commercial boats for sightseeing and fishing. Right now, things are slow, but by spring break it will be a whole different story."

"Belle? She runs the ranch?" Her expression shifted, and Hudson couldn't read it. Something was up.

"Yeah. She's been in charge of the Diamondback since Xavier's father passed away a couple of years ago. Xavier was out of the country at the time."

Abigail's eyes went wide. "He's..." Her head dropped. "He died? I'm so sorry." The words were mumbled.

Selena took a step forward and put her hand on Abigail's arm. "Are you okay?"

Lifting her eyes, she nodded. The biggest, fakest smile he had ever seen was spread wide across her face. "I'm sorry to hear about your father-in-law. Um. It's cold and I need to get Paloma inside."

"Oh yeah. Sorry, I've kept you out here so long. It was nice meeting you. If there is anything I can do to help..." Selena was already talking to Abigail's back.

"Welcome to Port Del Mar," she said to herself before turning to Hudson. "What happened? That turned weird really fast, right? Or am I being too sensitive?"

"She's had an extremely hard time of it lately, and she feels guilty that her daughter got sick. She probably just realized she should get her inside. But I'll follow up and make sure everything is okay."

"I don't know." She looked after the red coat swinging around Abigail's knees. "I see what you mean by something being off." Turning back to him, she grinned. "I'll trust you to find out anything that needs to be found out. And about the mischief and vandalism in town, let's call in our community teen task force for an emergency meeting tomorrow, and we can give this new problem a solid study before it gets out of hand."

They shared a smile. "I'll be there." The committee of town busy bodies loved the important sounding title to their group.

"You might want to go check on your girl. I'll see you later."

"She's not my girl or anything else. Just part of my job."

"Uh-huh. You keep telling yourself that."

"As I mentioned before, she has some issues she's running from, which means they might be following. My number one priority is to protect this community."

She laughed. "I never doubted that, but I don't think it's the community you're worried about with the way you were watching that door. Relax, Sheriff. It's okay... you have every right to a personal life. But be careful. No one knows anything about her."

"It's not personal." He sighed. He didn't have the time or attention to give to a life outside of his daughter or his job right now. But he did need to find out why Abigail was acting so strangely.

He thought back to their conversation about the De La Rosas. Why was she asking so many questions about them? They were a hardworking family, and they didn't need any more trouble delivered to their door. No matter how pretty the package was.

Her father was dead.

The world blurred around her, and she headed in the direction of the *panadería*. What was wrong with her knees? They were going numb. She put her free hand on the door and tried to open it, but she wasn't strong enough.

Desperation clawed at her heart. She needed to process what was happening. Of all the possible scenarios, it had never occurred to her that the giant of a man she remembered as her father would be dead.

Stumbling into the homey bakery, she reached out to brace herself on the wall. She scanned the area for a safe place to sit. It was hard to focus, but if she stayed on her feet any longer, she'd be sick. A few people lingered, but thankfully the morning rush was over.

Margarita came over and pulled her into a chair.

"Thank you," she managed to say. As much as she wanted to protest, she wasn't sure she would be able to get Paloma and herself up the stairs without collapsing.

My father is gone forever. He will never be able to explain why he abandoned me.

How could he be dead? Her brothers or cousins hadn't bothered to reach out and tell her? Memories of Belle doing her hair and helping her pick out clothes to pack flooded her mind. Belle ran the ranch now. Had they planned to send her away? She just needed a moment to get her legs back under her, then she'd go upstairs. Her brothers Xavier and Damian were in town. What about Elijah? He'd been with Belle when they gave her to their great-aunt. Had they all wanted to get rid of her?

The last few days had been great. The Espinozas had reassured her that she could take the time she needed to make sure Paloma was healthy and strong, then they would talk about the apartment and job...

"Abigail!" Margarita exclaimed from across the little table. The oldest sister grabbed her upper arm. "What's wrong, *mija*? Is it Paloma?"

"No." Her baby girl had just gotten a good report from the doctor, but Abigail didn't want to talk to anyone right now. She had come to Port Del Mar hoping to find family and friends; she hadn't wanted to be alone any longer. Now all she wanted was to be invisible.

"Why do you look as if you've lost your best friend? Did the doctor tell you something bad?"

"I'm fine. Paloma is great. We won't know what caused the seizure and she might not ever have one again. For now, we're healthy and safe. Now that I know she's fine, I think everything has finally caught up with me. I just need a bit of time to myself. You and your family have been so generous, and I don't know why." She squeezed her eyes shut, but it didn't stop the tears. "I'll never be able to repay you."

"Oh, *mija*. We all need help every now and then. We're God's hands and heart. We're happy to help you. Mom has brought over a highchair she had at the house. I have a bag of baby clothes and a few other things donated by the church. Do you want us to bring them later?"

She wiped her face with the back of her hand. How had she missed the big colorful bag on the floor between them? "Sorry. I'm a total mess. That's fine."

"No apologies. I'll find someone to help get the stuff out of my car, then I'll leave you alone. We can talk later. Do you need help getting up the stairs?"

"No. I'm—"

"I'll take the bag and Paloma." The deep voice from behind was like a jolt to her heart. What she didn't know was whether it was a lifesaving shock or a warning of danger.

"Come on. Let's get you upstairs." He gathered the bag from the floor and looped it over his shoulder, then took Paloma from her and tucked the baby into the crook of his arm. She looked so natural there.

Without saying another word, he held out his free hand to help her up, then headed to the back door.

The bag was so big but he made carrying it and Paloma look so easy. That's what fathers did, right? They carried the burdens when life got too heavy.

Part of the blanket had slipped down, and Paloma's tiny hand grabbed at his lips. He grinned and made faces at her.

In her head, Abigail had created an imaginary father holding his granddaughter for the first time and falling in love with her, unable to resist her charms.

But her father was gone. Dead. She'd never get to see him, be held in a big bear hug or hear his voice. See him with Paloma. Not ever.

Hudson paused at the back door and waited for her. The few customers that were in the bakery stared with open curiosity. She couldn't think about them right now. The upstairs apartment offered her sanctuary. If she could get behind the door, then she could safely fall apart again. Would life ever get easier?

Head high and gut pulled in tight, she followed Hudson and her daughter. She hadn't had a father in a long time; this news shouldn't change anything for her. She blinked as her eyes started to burn.

Paloma was healthy and happy. That's what mattered most, not the death of a man she barely remembered. It was just the end of a dream, one of many she'd had over the years. Dreams came and went. It was time to get a new and better one.

God had her. He was her true Father, the One that had her in His arms and would never let her go, even when she turned from Him. With a nod to herself, she climbed the steps.

Hudson struggled with the door a bit, but finally opened it and went inside. Stepping into the apartment, Abigail felt a new calmness wash over her. She didn't need the family that threw her away. The Espinozas could become her family if they'd have her. Maybe God had brought her to Port Del Mar, not for the father that abandoned her, but for these wonderful people who had truly reached out and helped a stranger for no other reason than being genuinely nice.

Kneeling, Hudson eased Paloma into the little playpen and waved a floppy pony at her. Giggling, she reached for her favorite toy and hugged it close. A little drool slipped down her chin as she chewed on the front leg.

He twisted so he could see Abigail over his shoulder. "Looks like someone's teething." He stood, then turned fully to her. "What's going on? Was it the appointment? Did the doctor give you bad news?" His expression was grim as he straightened. Was being with her the worst thing he had to do today? Or maybe, like her, he was tired. As a single dad and sheriff, the responsibilities had to be never-ending.

"It looks as if she had a strong reaction to an ear infection. And as I told the PA during the first visit, since she didn't run a fever, I didn't even know she was sick. So her body kind of did a shut-down thing. Everyone must think I'm a horrible mother. Maybe I am."

He studied her for a moment, a piercing stare. The urge to squirm tightened her muscles, but she held still. He finally moved his gaze and looked down at her daughter. "I would face a hundred hungry bobcats over my daughter being sick ever again. It's hard."

She nodded. Was he going to interrogate her now? "Thank you for helping us up the stairs. I'm still a little tired."

With a serious nod, he moved past her. He was leaving. She swatted the disappointment away. This was good. Him leaving was good.

But he didn't go to the door. Instead, he went to her refrigerator and pulled out one of the dishes Mrs. Espinoza had left. Taking off the cover and putting a paper towel over it, he popped it into the microwave. Then he put a couple of tortillas on the cast-iron skillet.

"You need to eat."

"I'm good." Why were they always trying to feed her? Crossing her arms over her chest, she tried to think of a reason to turn him down. Her stomach rumbled. *Great timing.*

A corner of his mouth quirked up, but he was polite enough not to make a comment about the noise her tummy made.

"The way you ended the conversation with Mayor

De La Rosa was weird. Something happened. What was said that changed your mood so drastically?"

Heat climbed her neck, and it was hard to focus. "I don't know what you're talking about."

They stared at each other in silence. Making sure her breathing stayed steady, Abigail lifted her chin as if she didn't have anything to hide. She didn't. Her father was none of the sheriff's business.

The beeping of the timer pulled his gaze from her. With his back to her, she allowed her shoulders to fall. She was a horrible liar. Could she tell him? How well did she know the De La Rosa family?

He placed the bowl on the table and went back for the tortillas. "Sit and have a bite to eat." One more trip and he had the plate loaded with shredded lettuce, onions, lime, chilis and radishes.

She blinked at the table. No one, since her mother, had made a meal just for her—or even toasted bread. Now she had the Espinozas and Hudson cooking for her every time she turned around. "Why are you feeding me?"

He sighed and sat at the table. "Like I said, you need nourishment. And Maria told me she had her pozole up here. So, I'm making sure you eat, which means I get to eat it too." Spooning a good helping of the chicken pozole into both of their bowls, he topped his with everything but the onions.

She sat across the table and watched him. The food smelled so good, but she wasn't hungry. Hadn't been for a while now.

He lifted his spoon to her before taking a bite.

Why was he doing this? She didn't understand his motivation. There had to be a reason he was being so nice to her. If nothing else, this was easier than thinking about her father being gone forever.

He pushed the garnishes toward her. "I promise you are about to have the best pozole this side of the border."

Finally acquiescing, she swished her spoon in the soup.

"How about you tell me what happened outside with Mayor De La Rosa."

She shook her head and took a bite. He was right— it was delicious. "I don't know. It's been too much, and it all hit me. I guess knowing Paloma was okay just let everything else hit me at once. Please tell the mayor I'm so sorry if I acted weird."

"Don't worry about her. She and Xavier, her husband, have triplets. I'm sure she understands being overwhelmed as a parent."

"*Triplets?* Wow. How old are they? Do you know them well? The De La Rosas?"

"I consider Xavier one of my best friends. The boys are somewhere between three and four. The De La Rosas are good people. Why so many questions about them?"

She shrugged and took another bite to avoid answering right away. Xavier had triplets. What were their names? Did Damian, Belle or Elijah have kids?

Belle and Elijah were her cousins, but her mother had taken them in and raised them. Did their mother ever come back? Did the others have children? That would make her an aunt.

Did they know about her, or had she been wiped from the family history? So many questions burned through her mind. Why didn't they find her to tell her that her father had died?

This wonderful lunch would be wasted on her. It would sit in her stomach like boulders. She looked up, and her gaze collided with Hudson's.

Quickly she turned away. What was blazing in those brilliant eyes of his? She shouldn't care. She didn't.

If she repeated that enough, it would become true. Maybe. There were definitely more important items on her list of things to worry about.

"Their names have come up several times, and then I find out the mayor is related to them. I don't know. I'd rather talk about other people and their families than my lack of one. Big families interest me. I always wanted one." That was the truth. She sighed, and he kept staring at her.

If she was smart, she'd keep quiet. Shifting to the side, she looked over her shoulder at Paloma playing with her toys. He was waiting for her to say more.

With a deep breath, she decided to tell him the truth. Some of it, anyway. "When people find out who I am—who my husband is—will they be as friendly? I can't even keep my daughter safe." Even just a part of the truth was hard. She would *not* cry…

"None of that is your fault." His deep voice right next to her caused her to jump. When had he moved to her side? He was close enough to her for his clean, masculine scent to tickle her nose. It was so warm and comforting, like fresh rain and cut grass. She lowered her head and bit her bottom lip.

At the slight touch of his hand on her shoulder, her nerves scrambled, then settled quickly. Determined, she warned herself not to lean on him. She had to learn to take care of herself and not wait for others to save her. It only made things worse.

He didn't stay by her side for long. Shifting back, he slid into the chair next to hers.

"As parents, all we can do is our best and leave the rest up to God. Children get sick whether you stay in one place or travel. Would she have been better growing up where everyone knew who her father was?" He looked over at Paloma playing on the floor. "You get to tell her your story in your own time and way. Your instincts were right about leaving Cincinnati. You both need a new start. You can write the next chapter of your story."

There was a long moment of silence, then he turned to her. "Not many people know, but one of the reasons I took the opportunity to be sheriff in Port Del Mar was to give my daughter a clean slate. She wouldn't hear rumors about her mom. I get to control our narrative. Each year, I tell her a little more." He shrugged. "Some stuff I'll never tell her."

He nodded as if he were having another conversation she couldn't hear. "We love our children, and every day as parents we have to make choices that can bury us in self-doubt. At those times, I rely heavily on my faith that God has her, even when I mess up. Most of us try our best, but we're flawed. God is always perfect."

He looked so serious, but he hadn't met her gaze once while telling her about his daughter. What was his story? "Is her mother in prison?"

"No." His half smile softened his face. "Nothing like that. She wanted a life she thought I would give her. When she discovered I wanted to stay in law enforcement, she left. She walked out and didn't look back. Hasn't even reached out to Charlotte in six years."

"I can't imagine a mother doing that. I'm sorry."

"For her, a baby had been a means to an end. When she didn't get the ending she wanted, she moved on. As an adult, I can handle it. Mostly." He gave her a lopsided grin. "But kids don't understand. On the plus side, it all happened before Charlotte was old enough to remember. I get to explain it to her. You'll get to do the same with Paloma."

"I don't know how to make what her father did easier to hear. Or the mistakes I made. I don't want her to ever feel lost or abandoned." Pressing her lips closed, she cut off her verbal outpouring. He was a stranger and didn't need to know her issues.

"You lost your family as a kid." It was a statement. He tilted his head and studied her. "You told Maria you were nine?"

The lump in her throat stopped her from saying anything.

With a grim expression, he nodded. "The trauma of losing family when you're older is harder to deal with. The scars are in our memories and run deeper. That can affect us as adults."

Her heart clenched. Was he hinting that he knew she was back in town to reconnect with a family that might not want her?

The colorful place mat was a good diversion. Tracing the aqua line with her finger, Abigail studied the zigzag design. At first it looked random, but she found the intricate pattern.

Was there a pattern to her life she wasn't seeing?

He stood. "Maria asked me to bring up a few more things that she found. There's more bedding." Without waiting for her to reply, he left the apartment.

Abigail was overwhelmed with emotion and needed

to be close to her baby. Across from the playpen with her back to the sofa, she stared at her daughter.

Her beautiful baby girl had fallen asleep, lost in innocent dreams. "You're never going to meet your grandpa." At their rate she might not meet any of her family.

She swallowed a lump in her throat and nearly choked on the sob that wanted to escape. Pulling her knees against her chest, she tightened her whole body into a ball. Hugging herself tight, she tried to stop the tears. It didn't work. Losing complete control, she felt the sobs take over. They came one on top of another, making her whole body ache.

Thankfully, Paloma was still fast asleep. Abigail pulled the quilt off the back of the couch and cocooned herself inside. She couldn't stop the trembles that overtook her body.

Had God brought her all this way for nothing but more heartbreak? She was so tired of hurting. All she wanted to do was sleep, but she couldn't. What if her baby girl needed her and she didn't hear her?

Hudson would be back soon. She had to get herself under control. Forcing deep breaths, she finally reduced the sobs to snuffles.

The sheriff had said to trust God. But how? Every time she trusted that things would get better, life kicked her in the gut. She couldn't let this happen to her baby girl.

But how could she protect her? What if something happened to her? Who would be there for her daughter? They had no one. The Espinozas had taken them in, but they were just a charity case, not real family.

A tear fell on the back of her hand. With a deep

breath, she relaxed the death grip she had on the quilt and wiped her face dry.

Most of her memories were shadows, but she remembered her father riding on his horse. He had been so tall and handsome in his cowboy hat. Her mother had said she fell in love at first sight when she saw him at a rodeo.

Why were her memories so fuzzy? She couldn't even remember his voice.

Now she would never hear it again. She had thought that if she could get to Texas, her father would be here. In her dreams, her father would step in and fix everything that was wrong.

She had met Xavier's wife. They had triplets. What about her brother Damian or her cousin Belle? Then there was her cousin Elijah, he had looked so much like her father. He was always outside, but he had a smile for her every time she saw him. Or was she making up the memories she wanted? What if she had it all wrong?

Xavier. He had picked her up from school. She had loved her big brother so much and had looked up to him. That couldn't be made up, could it?

Xavier took her riding over the ranch. He had promised to take care of her.

At first, her faith had been unyielding. He would come for her. Belle too. Under her bed, the small overnight bag they had sent her off with was packed and ready for when they knocked on the door. They had said they loved her and would always protect her.

It took her a couple of years to reach the conclusion that they had lied. Why were they keeping her away from the ranch? Was it greed? Maybe they were fighting over the ranch and didn't want her around to take a piece. But she didn't care about the land or any inheritance. She just wanted her family.

A family that might only live in her dreams.

A half sob slipped through. No. She didn't want to cry anymore, but what she wanted had never mattered before.

The door handle jiggled. She pulled the quilt over her head and stifled any lingering cries. If she was quiet, he'd think she went to sleep and go away.

Chapter Seven

Hudson shifted the highchair so he could open the door. The knob was stuck. He'd have to get his tools and fix that before he left. What else needed to be done? Out of habit, he started a mental list of items Abigail might still need.

He liked lists. They gave him a sense of order and control in a world that turned chaotic at the turn of a knob. Yes. Lists were good. Even better when items were checked off. Best feeling in the world.

He put his shoulder to the wood to create a push-and-pull action.

Why was he even bothering making plans to fix her door? He couldn't imagine Abigail being satisfied with the bare minimum for long. She had grown accustomed to a certain lifestyle. The apartment was cozy and had the basics, but how much longer would it be before she grew restless and missed the glamorous homes and restaurants?

He gritted his teeth. Why was he making it his problem?

He had enough self-awareness to know he had issues

with women who needed saving. Or, at least, who were good at acting the part. As soon as he put this highchair together, he was out of here.

But first, he had to get into the apartment. Had she locked him out?

Out of pure frustration, he put his full weight behind one last shove. The door gave, and he almost lost his balance. Inside, he froze. There was a tension in the room that had his spine stiffening.

It was too quiet. Then he heard a muffled sound, as if someone had just finished a hard cry but was trying to hide. Then it was quiet again. Had he imagined the sob?

He wasn't sure. His ex-wife always made sure he knew she was crying. It was her best performance. She had been enormously proud of her ability to produce real tears on command.

Crossing the room, he glanced into the crib. Paloma was in a deep sleep, stretched out with both arms over her head in a picture of total contentment. Her round little face was turned to the side, and she made soft sucking noises.

Not the source of the stifled sobs.

Where was Abigail? Something was wrong. She wouldn't have left her daughter alone. She had barely allowed him to hold her. Setting the box against the wall, he turned to go down the hall when he spotted the bundle on the floor behind the sofa. The quilt trembled.

Had Abigail passed out again? Blood pounded in his ears as his heart rate increased. He knelt next to the small mound and laid his hand on the corner closest to him. He thought it was her head, but he wasn't sure.

Maybe she was hiding on purpose and didn't want anyone to see her. But he couldn't leave her like this.

Frustration roiled through him. Why was he working so hard to justify staying and getting involved? It was a waste of time because he knew he was just going to do it anyway, even though it would be breaking his rule about getting involved with women in trouble.

But this was for the baby. Really, who would just walk out knowing that a mom was in no condition to care for a helpless baby? He eased further down so that he wouldn't be looming over her when he pulled the cover back.

"Abigail? It's Hudson. Sheriff Menchaca." He could at least try to keep it professional. "Are you okay? Should I call Margarita or Resa?"

She made a noise that might have meant to be no, but he wasn't sure. Gently, he pulled back the pink-and-purple-patched quilt. He hadn't even known there were that many shades of pink.

Her stylish blond cut had become a mess. He still couldn't see her face. What wasn't covered by her hair was buried in her hands. It was the most heartbreaking sight he had seen in a long time. It pulled on every string attached to his stupid heart.

After years in his line of work and one disastrous marriage, there should be no strings left to yank. He had worked hard to be detached in these types of situations. What was it about Abigail Dixon that brought out the protector in him?

Everything inside him begged to pull her into his arms and promise to make it better. But he knew reaching for her was a bad idea. Instead, his free hand went to his phone. "Abigail, I'm going to call Margarita. They'll be up in a minute to help." Then he could escape, knowing that she was not alone.

That was the best plan for them all.

"No." She popped up, her hand reaching for his. The warm skin was soft. He could have easily broken the contact, but he didn't. "Abigail, you need help."

She sat up, moving away from him as she pushed her hair out of her face. "Please don't. The idea that anyone else will see me like this is too mortifying. Please. Just leave. I'll be all right. It was just a moment. Just like after a crisis, when everything calms down. You know? The adrenaline rush that pushed you through crashes."

He did get that. "Okay. Even more of a reason for someone to come stay so you can get some good sleep in the bed. Not on the floor next to your daughter's playpen."

"No. I'm good now." Standing, she moved to sit on the sofa, pulling the quilt behind her.

"Hudson, I was so close to being homeless with a sick baby. But we have this lovely apartment, and she's healthy." She turned to look at the sleeping baby. "She doesn't have a worry in the world. It just hit me. Everyone's kindness has been too much. I'm not used to people being nice just to be nice. It was a little meltdown. It's over. I'm so sorry you had to witness it." With a deep sigh, she relaxed her shoulders and smiled at him. "I'm good to go. You can leave. Thank you for everything."

Not taking his gaze off hers, he sat on the opposite corner of the couch.

"Leaving you by yourself at this point might not be the smartest move."

"Paloma is napping. I just need a little nap too."

"On the floor? You are beyond exhausted. You've been through a life-changing event and then your daughter became sick while you were basically living out of your car. You need real rest."

With a lopsided smile, she chuckled. *"Life-changing event.* That's the nicest way I've heard it put. But you're right. My ex-husband being caught stealing millions of innocent people's retirement funds is a life-changing event. For so many people."

She looked down, twisting her lips. "There is so much wrong with everything he did, and I lived off the benefits." Palms pressed together and fingers intertwined, she pressed her knuckles to her forehead. "I didn't know about any of it, but I was there with him. Do you know he never apologized? No remorse. The last time we talked, he was worried about how he would survive without his houses, cars and boats. What he didn't understand is that those weren't his. They belonged to the people he stole from. How could I be married to a man like that? Maybe I deserve all the hate and the messed-up life, but Paloma doesn't." She shook her head and wrapped her arms around her middle. She looked down at her hands as her messy hair fell around her face.

He sat, letting her vent. He was sure she hadn't had anyone to really talk to. This was probably the first time she had put her fear and anger into words.

And, honestly, he had judged her a bit too. Some of those thoughts had been his.

"I'm sorry for dropping this on you. Please forget I said any of that. You're right. I'm exhausted."

He leaned closer to her, not touching but needing to let her know he was there. "Just so you know. Everything you say stays between us." She looked so lost and alone. He wanted to see her smile. So he gave her a grin and winked. "Unless you start confessing to crimes, then I'm obligated to arrest you."

"I would have a place to stay and three meals a day." With a huff, she flopped her head back and looked at the ceiling. "How sad is that? If it wasn't for Paloma, I would make something up just to have a place to be. Maybe she would be better off without me."

"You don't mean that."

She sighed. "Only three days and you know me so well." She turned her head and looked at her daughter. "As long as she has me, she'll have all the love in the world—but is it enough if I can't keep her safe?"

"When I talk to parents that are going through a traumatic event, I have a piece of advice I always give. As a good parent, your instinct is to take care of your child first." This time he did reach out and waited for her to meet his gaze and take his hand.

For a split second, she looked him in the eye, then looked away again. "I'm not sure bad choices count as traumatic events. So many people say I deserve even more..." She closed her eyes and pulled her lips between her teeth.

If she was putting on a show to pull him in, it was working. He flexed his hand, inviting her to take it.

Abigail hesitated. Taking ahold of his hand would mean she was accepting his help. How would she learn to stand on her own if she kept letting others step in and take care of her?

His hand stayed in place. With her stomach in knots, she allowed her fingertips to make contact.

He released a deep breath, some of the tension leaving his shoulders. "She needs you whole and healthy.

Physically and mentally." His fingers rolled around hers, surrounding her hand with a light touch. When was the last time someone had touched her with gentleness, for no other reason than to reassure her and comfort her?

He lowered his chin and held her gaze. "You've traveled, right? In an airplane they tell you to get your oxygen mask on first. Then it's safe to take care of your child. If you pass out, you aren't any good to the people counting on you."

"Think of me as your oxygen mask." He stood and offered his hand again. "I'm temporary until the cabin pressure is stabilized. Take a few deep breaths, eat, take a nap. Then I'll be gone, and you can take care of your daughter."

Was she being tested? At what point was she going to truly be independent and stand on her own without needing oxygen? "But when do I start breathing on my own? I can't keep relying on someone to come along and save me. The highchair is not that complicated. I've got this. I'm good."

"I'll get the last of the bags out of Margarita's car. Come on. You didn't eat much. Get some food in your system then take a short nap while I put the highchair together. Then you'll have enough oxygen to take care of yourself and your daughter. And I'll leave you all alone, okay?"

Her sight blurred. Her father would not be coming to her rescue, but God had sent the sheriff today.

It wouldn't undermine her independence to accept his help. It was temporary, right? Putting her hand in his, she allowed him to lift her to her feet. He pulled out a chair for her. The room was silent as she dug into the pozole. This time she savored the home-cooked meal that had been made for her. It was the best thing she had eaten since her mother had cooked for her.

Closing her eyes, she sank into the moment and allowed the warmth of their care to pour into her.

Hudson chuckled. Her eyes shot open. Had she moaned or made some other embarrassing noise?

He was at the door. "I told you it was good. There's more on the stove if you finish that before I'm back."

Forcing her spoon down, she looked up at him. "Thank you. I appreciate you not saying anything to the sisters. They already tend to hover and worry."

Halfway through the door, he turned back to her. "I know you're trying to be independent and strong, but they don't have an agenda. They're good people, and my job is to protect them from their own generosity."

Was he warning her or comforting her? Either way she was too tired to argue. She tried to give him an agreeable expression, but her lips were tight. Everyone had an agenda. Including the sheriff. With one last frown as if suspicious of her fake smile, he walked out the door.

Chapter Eight

The sun had not yet made an appearance over the Gulf and Paloma was sound asleep in the portable crib they had set up by the back door. They had fallen into a nice routine with the sisters over the last week and half.

"Josefina!" Abigail called from the front as soon as she put the phone down. "New order. The Wimberly Cattle Company needs two dozen empanadas for tomorrow morning." She wrote the order in the spiral notebook the women kept at the register. "Half pumpkin, half strawberry." With the sharp pencil, she wrote the amount in another ledger that contained the regular customer accounts.

She should talk them into letting her update their system. It could be streamlined online. Orders placed and completed, along with payments in one place on their website. Which was another whole issue.

If they would let her update everything, Margarita wouldn't have to take paperwork home or come back at night to reconcile the accounts. It was as though they didn't live in the twenty-first century.

The first time they showed her how they took orders, tracked them and collected payments, she was floored. She didn't know anyone who did business like this anymore.

Margarita bustled in from the back, adding to the stack of boxes on the front counter. Three girls came in the back door. Angie and Nica were Margarita's two oldest, and Desirae was Josefina's only child. "Good morning, Ms. Abigail." They seemed too cheerful for the crack of dawn. Behind them came Josh, Margarita's youngest at eight. He looked as if he'd just been pulled out of bed and was not happy about the upright position.

They each took a stack of white boxes of preordered pastries to load into Jose's truck.

"The labels are on the top," Margarita explained every morning, but they nodded as if they'd never been told a million times. She took the last stack and reminded Abigail as she took them to the waiting truck. "Don't forget to put the order in the ledger so I can bill them."

"I got it. You know, this could all be done online. Your customers could place the orders and make a payment at the same time. You would have time to make more product." They sold out every day.

"Oh, people like the personal touch. And having you answering the morning phones has already increased our productivity."

"They'd still get the special treatment—it would just be more organized…" The last few words trailed off. The oldest sister was already out the door. Jose, Margarita's husband, and the kids would make the early morning deliveries, and then he would drop the kids off at school before heading to his garage. They were such a hardworking family, and Abigail knew that if they let her, they could work a little less hard.

It had been two weeks, but Abigail knew without a doubt that coming to Port Del Mar had been a God thing.

She had mistakenly assumed it was to reconnect with her family and find out why they had sent her away, then forgotten her.

But finding out her father was dead had rattled the foundation of everything she thought she knew. Her brothers and cousins didn't want her back. With her father gone, there was no reason to even tell them she was in town. No reason to set herself up to be rejected by them again.

Every time thoughts of what-if crowded her mind, she quoted Hebrew 13:6. *So that we may boldly say, The Lord is my helper, and I will not fear what man shall do unto me.*

It was posted on her bathroom mirror.

The phone rang again. As she picked it up, Josefina came from the kitchen. Smiling as she hummed a song, she put a stack of folded boxes featuring the bakery's logo under the counter, then rushed back to the kitchen. Then Margarita came in and did her morning routine. She checked all the tables and arranged the books on the shelves, then flipped the Open sign and unlocked the door.

Just like every morning since Abigail had joined them, there was a small group of people outside, waiting to come in and start their day with a perfect cup of coffee and their favorite pastry.

Abigail was convinced it was the Espinoza family's

love seeped into every recipe and coating every square inch of the shop that made the difference.

How the Espinozas had surrounded her in a warm *familia* blanket of love still mystified her. At times it made her so uncomfortable that her instinct was to run.

She had no experience with this type of attention. As nice as it was, it also stressed her out. What would happen next? Something this good never lasted long.

Margarita greeted everyone and served them at the counter, then they would come to Abigail to pay. This morning, as per usual, Hudson was one of the first to come into the bakery. Sometimes he had an order to pick up, but other days he sat down to have his breakfast here. A few times, like today, he brought Charlotte with him.

Abigail's nerves went all wobbly and tingly. *Settle down, he's just getting breakfast.*

It wasn't like he went out of his way to talk to her. Over a week had passed since they'd spent any time alone together. Hudson said he would leave her alone, and he had stuck to his word. He barely talked to her now. A polite "good morning" and "thank you" was the extent of their conversation.

This morning, Charlotte pressed her face to the front of the glass, searching for the blueberry cake doughnut.

"We had a big order of your favorites this morning," Margarita told her. "A new batch will be coming out of the oven soon. Do you want to wait for hot fresh doughnuts or pick something else? The cinnamon twist was just put out. Do you want one of those?"

She shook her head, then looked up at her dad. "Can I wait for the blueberry ones?"

Glancing at his watch, he nodded. "We've got time."

He moved to stand in front of her and handed over his card. "Morning." He smiled at Paloma standing in her playpen talking to people. "Looks as if she is settling in."

Before she could reply, he turned to the opening door. "Xavier," he called out, with a warm smile for the man who walked in.

Her stomach took a nosedive. *Xavier.* Not breathing, she tucked her head down. Was it her brother? She was afraid to look up. What if it was and he recognized her? Every muscle in her body tightened. What if he didn't? That would be worse.

Twisting her head just enough to see him out of the corners of her eyes, she peered at the man Hudson was now having a conversation with. Words slipped past their moving lips, but she couldn't hear a sound.

It was him. Her brother. Sweet memories of Xavier defending her at school, helping her tie her shoes and teaching her to ride bombarded her. He had been her hero.

He was bigger now, a grown man. Selena had said he'd been out of the country. Had he joined the military? After the weird way she had acted around Selena, she'd been afraid to ask any questions.

Now there were a ton.

"Abigail?" Hudson called her name.

Blinking to clear her thoughts, she looked at him. "Yes?" she somehow managed.

"Is there a problem with my card?" He leaned over to look at the scanner.

"Oh. Um…it's the machine." She had taken so long that it had canceled the transaction. "This thing is so old."

Xavier laughed. "I'm surprised they even take credit cards. The sisters are a little old-school."

Nodding, Hudson grinned. "Hey, at least they upgraded from the old carbon-copy machine."

She handed him his card. "Here you go. Sorry about that."

Xavier held out his hand. "Since my friend here is rude, I'll have to introduce myself. I'm Xavier De La Rosa. You met my wife, Selena."

She. Could. Not. Breathe. Her gaze darted to his hand, then to his face. He didn't know who she was.

"Abigail?" Hudson leaned closer, his forehead wrinkled with heavy frown lines. "Are you okay?"

Pull it together. He was going to think she was having another breakdown. She took Xavier's outreached hand. "Sorry, too early in the morning. Paloma didn't sleep well last night."

Hudson twisted to look at Paloma, who was carrying on a conversation, showing her cloth book to a customer. "Is she okay? Any setbacks?"

"No. Just a normal, mommy-I-want-to-play-now type of night." She wiped her hand on her jeans and avoided any eye contact with her brother. She knew she had changed a lot since she was nine. There was the growth spurt, and her hair was blond with a completely different style. And then there was the weight. She wasn't the chubby little sister he had known. But still, shouldn't there be something, like a do-I-know-you-from-somewhere kind of recognition?

The bell rang and new customers came in, pushing the two men in front of her to move on.

Xavier lifted his coffee. "Nice meeting you. It's a small town, so I'm sure I'll be seeing you around." He turned to Hudson. "Will you join me? I have some questions."

"Sure." They went to a table by the front window. Charlotte took a book out of her backpack.

"Ma'am?"

Abigail jumped. She stopped gawking at Hudson and helped the next customer. Whenever she had a second, her gaze slipped to the table by the big window. She wasn't sure if it was Xavier or Hudson who kept pulling her attention away.

When Josefina brought out a tray of the hot blueberry cake doughnuts, she set one to the side. "Is Ms. Charlotte waiting for this?"

Margarita was laughing with a mom who had a couple of kids with her, and Josefina rushed back to the kitchen. Taking a deep breath, Abigail picked up the little plate. She could do this without acting weird.

Provided she didn't blurt out any off-the-wall questions. Hudson was already worried about her state of mind. When she was halfway to the table, Xavier stood.

"Thanks for your help. I have an early appointment on the dock. See you." Then he turned and left without a glance at her.

He was gone.

For a moment, she had the ridiculous sense of being abandoned all over again. She just stood there and watched as Xavier walked across the street.

"Ms. Abigail, is that mine?" Charlotte was politely standing next to her.

Forcing a smile, she handed the girl her breakfast. "Yes, it is." Raising her eyes to meet Hudson's was a mistake.

The wrinkled forehead was unmistakable evidence

that he had questions about her odd behavior. Again. Lifting her chin, she nodded to him.

He raised one brow. What did *that* mean?

She couldn't look away. For a long moment, they stared at each other, then his phone went off and he looked away.

That was a win for her, right?

He stood and glanced around, then stepped closer to her. "I need to take this outside. Would you keep an eye on Charlotte?"

"Of course." She slipped into the chair he had just left and turned to his daughter. "Was the doughnut worth the wait?"

Cheeks full of blueberry goodness, the six-year-old nodded, her ponytail bobbing with her head. Today she wore a big purple bow.

She heard Paloma. "Little Miss Thing is ready for breakfast. Want to check on her with me?"

"Can I hold her?"

"You can help me keep her entertained while I make her bottle." Paloma smiled at them while she rubbed her eye with a tiny fist. With Charlotte talking to the baby, Abigail told Josefina that she was clocking out to feed Paloma.

She took Charlotte and Paloma to the family booth in the back of the kitchen. With the little girl sitting close to her, she let her give the baby her bottle.

Hudson came in and scanned the room for his daughter. Seeing her, his shoulders relaxed, then he turned to Josefina, who was filling and folding individual empanadas. "Josefina, I need some help. There's an incident on the other side of town, and I need to go now. Would you be able to take Charlotte to school in thirty minutes?"

"I'm sorry, but I can't. Margarita and I have a couple of special orders. One's a wedding. Maybe Abigail could. Abigail, would you be able to take her?"

"Sure. That's not a problem. I just need directions to the school." She pulled her bottom lip between her teeth. "If that's okay with you, Sheriff. I don't mind. I'm a careful driver."

"Yes!" Charlotte said. "That would be fun. I can help with the baby, then she can take me to school. My teacher would love to meet Paloma. Can she pick me up too?"

Her large eyes turned to Abigail. "Mrs. Johnson watches me when Daddy has work, but her mom got real sick yesterday. Daddy wants me to go to the afterschool camp. But I don't want to. Cody goes and he's mean."

"Charlotte." Hudson's voice had a sharp edge Abigail hadn't heard before.

"I don't mind. Paloma loves her. I can pick her up from school and bring her here or take her home and wait for you."

"Please, Daddy."

Heaving a heavy sigh, he looked at his phone. "She can take you to school this morning. We will talk abou—"

"Thank you, Daddy!" Charlotte leaped on her dad, hugging him tight around his upper legs.

He snorted and rubbed the top of her head. "Don't worry about after school. I should be able to pick her up." He kissed her. "Love you, baby girl." Then he was gone.

Charlotte was eager to help stock the white bakery bags at the front counter, and then she played with Paloma while Abigail helped a few customers.

Abigail lost track of time. She checked on the girls. They were still playing, giggling at a silly game Charlotte had made up. Her heart got the same gooey warm feeling she experienced when she watched a Hallmark movie. Margarita came out to the front with another tray.

"Hey, chica. You're going to be late if you don't get them babies in the car."

Checking her phone, Abigail gasped. How had thirty minutes slipped by so fast? She'd promised Hudson she would get his daughter to school on time and told him he could trust her.

He was going to think her irresponsible. She was pretty sure he already questioned her stability. She picked up Paloma and hustled Charlotte to the car.

When they pulled up to the drop-off spot, it was clear of cars. Of course, it was—they were late.

Putting the car in Park, she got Paloma out, then went around to help Charlotte out of the booster Margarita had given her. The little girl looked around, then up at Abigail. "Are we late? I'm never late."

"It's okay. I'll take you in and explain that it's my fault."

To get into the office, she had to press a button at the front door and explain who she was. They unlocked the door and she rushed through the lobby, ready to defend Charlotte and take the blame.

A dark-haired woman stood behind the long counter, and several others turned their way as they entered. A few seemed to drift out of the offices lining the hallway behind the counter. They were all doing something, but not really concentrating on their work. She recognized some of the faces from the bakery.

She pulled the girls closer to her, her heart slamming against her chest. Did they know about her husband, or were they merely curious as to why she had the sheriff's daughter?

"Hi, Mrs. Abernathy." Charlotte's voice was bright and cheery. "I was helping at the bakery this morning. Please don't tell Daddy I was late. This is Mrs. Dixon, she—"

"It's okay, Charlotte." Abigail put a hand on her shoulder. The six-year-old was trying to protect her. "I lost track of time. I'll let Hudson know it was my fault."

With a smirk, the brunette tilted her head. "Hudson, huh. Welcome to Port Del Mar, Mrs. Dixon. We hear the Espinoza sisters have let you move in above the bakery." She took a pink slip of paper off her desk and scribbled on it. "Here, Charlotte. Go on to class. Being tardy interrupts everyone's schedule. It's important to think of others, no matter who you are. Right, Mrs. Dixon?"

Abigail's stomach dropped. The woman knew who she was. That meant they all knew she was once married to Brady Dixon. That she had been the wife of a con man who stole other people's dreams.

Charlotte frowned for the first time. "But I wanted to introduce—"

"It's okay, Charlotte. She's right, class has already started. We can meet your teacher another day. You need to go on in."

Her little shoulders dropped. "Okay. Bye, Paloma." With a kiss on the baby's cheek and a quick hug around Abigail's waist, Charlotte disappeared.

The expressions on the faces of the women in the

front office ranged from sincere kindness to open hostility. Small towns were so strange. Was it because of her ex-husband, or had she read the room wrong? Had she made a mistake in using the sheriff's first name?

He had to be one of the most sought-after bachelors in Port Del Mar. Either way, they didn't know her, so she couldn't let their negativity take away the warm joy from her morning with Paloma and Charlotte.

With a tight smile, she left.

She finished out the morning at the counter, then took Paloma upstairs. It was time to take a deep dive into the sisters' website and explore all the possibilities that would make their business run more easily and their lives better.

This would be a good time to reestablish her own business and seek out more marketing work. She had managed to build a successful small business before her husband was arrested. Her clients had dropped her the minute word got out.

She couldn't blame them. With all the drama, she hadn't even tried to change their minds. The enormity of her husband's guilt had been too much for her to handle.

Port Del Mar was a new start, and it was time to build up a new clientele. A new name would be a good first step, but right now she didn't have the money to legally change it.

Would she go back to De La Rosa? This morning, she had come face-to-face with her oldest brother, and he hadn't even given her a second glance. She had always looked different from them, taking after her mother. Maybe she wasn't a De La Rosa. Was that the reason they had sent her away?

Nope, she wasn't even going to chase that proverbial rabbit down the hole. She had things to do. Things that she had control over and that mattered. First, the sisters' website, then some fresh branding for her and Paloma's new life.

Her daughter babbled in the back seat. "This is our fresh start, baby girl," Abigail told her.

She should forget about the De La Rosa family. They didn't know her or want her. They had obviously forgotten about her. The Espinozas, on the other hand, provided warmth and love to the whole community. Espinoza was a good name. So was Menchaca.

She shook her head. No. She was not going to fall into the trap of thinking that a man changing her name would save her.

Chapter Nine

Hudson's boots crunched the red gravel of his driveway. One hand on the smoothed railing, he paused before taking the stairs up to the beach house that he and Charlotte had called home for over a year now.

With each step, he mentally dropped the stress and ugliness of the day off his shoulders. Reaching the top of the landing, he turned and sat in the rocker. The wraparound deck had a couple of weathered rockers that had come with the house. He had added a cushioned bench and a table with six chairs. It was a great outdoor living space. They weren't on the beach, but they had a view of the ocean between the colorful houses that lined the other side of the street.

It was a restful home. The sounds of the waves allowed him to count his blessings and check in with God. On the gate, he had placed a verse his sisters had given him: *But the wisdom that is from above is first pure, then peaceable, gentle, and easy to be entreated, full of mercy and good fruits, without partiality, and without hypocrisy. And the fruit of righteousness is sown in peace of them that make peace.* James 3:17-18.

He was a peacemaker. It was his job, and today he had done his job to the best of his ability. Now he needed to let it all go and embrace all the love and joy his daughter brought him.

With his head cleared, he unlocked his door and stepped inside. His gaze narrowed. What had happened to his orderly living room?

It looked as if every blanket and sheet in the house now covered his furniture. It was a giant chaotic mess, and it put him on edge.

"Charlotte? Josefina?"

A gasp came from somewhere below the mess. "Daddy!" His daughter crawled out from under a side table and ran to him. The power of the small body colliding with his almost knocked him off-balance.

She wound her arms around him and buried her face against his pants leg. "You're home safe."

He picked her up and pulled her against him. Her heart was beating a mile a minute. "I'm sorry I'm late, sweetheart. I called Josefina…she said she'd make sure you'd get home."

His baby girl was crying now, her tears crushing him more than any physical blow could. He pulled her closer and pressed his lips against the side of her head. "It's okay. I'm home."

The blanket over the sofa was pushed back. To his surprise, Abigail Dixon stood up. "Someone at school told her about the incident that pulled you away this morning." She avoided his eye contact.

Squeezing him tighter, Charlotte nodded. "Cody told me a man was going to blow you up. He said his brother told him the man had guns and bombs."

She started crying again.

"Shh. I'm here. The man was upset, but he wasn't trying to hurt me. He wanted his wife's attention, and he wanted to hurt himself. We were there to protect his family and him. I was by my truck the whole time. That's what took so long. We didn't want anyone to get hurt. I'm so sorry, baby girl. You can't believe anything that Cody kid tells you." He wanted to talk to someone about this. That kid had been picking on his daughter for a while, but this was crossing the line.

"I told her you were going to be okay, and that Cody just had a big mouth. He sounds like a kid who likes to cause drama by talking about things he knows nothing about." Abigail's lips pressed into a hard line. "We've been staying busy. She's been fine for most of the night."

She looked as upset as his daughter.

"Thank you. Cody's older brother is a troublemaker in town, and his father isn't much better." He hadn't wanted to throw his weight around as sheriff, but that kid needed to leave his daughter alone.

"Cody says they're going to video Daddy harassing them," Charlotte told Abigail. Hudson had heard that threat from the family before.

Needing to change the subject, he walked over to Abigail and scanned the multicolored stronghold that covered his well-organized living room.

He had not expected any of this in his home. He put his free hand on his hip and tried to put a positive spin on it. Charlotte had been scared. Abigail had sacrificed his perfectly placed furniture for his daughter's sake. It had been a good call on her part.

"Wow. You built a big fort. It looks super strong."

Charlotte nodded against his chest. She was chewing on her thumb, something she hadn't done in over a year. "It is."

His heart broke. His job was to make the community safe—but was it at the expense of his daughter's mental health?

"I was scared, but Abigail prayed with me. She said when you got home, you'd be hungry after working so hard. We made dinner, then we took a bath and built a fort to hide inside until you got here. I told her you didn't like messes. That your rule is one toy at a time. But she said it would be okay. We got to show Paloma two of my favorite movies."

He glanced over at Abigail. She and Paloma had been the distraction his daughter needed.

Abigail crossed her arms over her middle and looked at his daughter. "Josefina thought Charlotte would feel better waiting for you at home. Charlotte has been a great help with Paloma, and she's a good cook. She helped make your favorite dinner."

"I did, and Ms. Josefina gave us some croissants with pecans and honey. She said after the pumpkin empanadas they were your favorite. They were sold out of all the empanadas."

Abigail had kept his daughter safe and had done everything she could to reassure her he'd be home. He treasured the feel of Charlotte's small body in his arms. In just a few years, she would be too big to hold like this. Kissing her head, he took in the smell of her apple shampoo.

"I love the honey croissants. The house smells like baked bread and lasagna." He set her down. "You said you made my favorite."

She took his hand and pulled him into the kitchen

area. "We did. After I helped bathe Paloma, we washed my hair. Abigail let me layer the pasta and cheese. She poured the sauce."

"You haven't eaten yet?" he asked. "It's past your bedtime."

"Abigail said you would be home, and I didn't want to eat without you. Can they stay the night? We could all camp in the fort. There are lots of pillows and blankets."

With her baby on her hip, Abigail was pulling the salad out of the refrigerator. "I've got to get Paloma home, but you and your dad both need to eat." She placed the bowl on the table, which was set with two plates, then went to the stove.

"Why are there only two plates?"

"I told her to get three plates." Charlotte made an I-told-you-so face at Abigail. "She said they would leave as soon as you got here. I think she should stay. She helped me cook it—she should eat it too."

"I agree. We had dinner with her, and now it's her turn to eat with us. Stay. Let me get the lasagna." He moved to the oven she had opened and took the hot pads from her. She nodded and grabbed the bread basket.

His daughter already had another plate on the table and was laying out silverware. "I told you Daddy would make you stay." Charlotte smiled at them, then climbed into her chair.

"I should go. Just let me gather the blankets and straighten up."

"Sit. Y'all made the meal together, so we will eat it together. The fort can stay up tonight."

"Really? Yay! Daddy, will you camp out with me?"

"Yes. Now let's pray so we can eat."

They all bowed their heads as he said a simple grace

over the food that was set before them. Afterward, Charlotte hit Abigail with a new knock-knock joke, and even Paloma laughed.

He grinned. This was nice. Sighing with contentment, he enjoyed the moment of feeling like a complete family. This was the dream he'd lost when his ex-wife had made it clear her wishes were so much grander than a simple family dinner. Zoe had been able to pretend for a while, but he had been too busy and self-absorbed and had missed the clues.

It was sad to realize that it wasn't Zoe he missed, but the feeling of returning to a family home where he could heal his heart after a difficult day in the world.

Zoe had not wanted the same things. He wanted to build what his parents had had before he got his mother killed.

Nope. Not going there. He closed his eyes and forced that ugly thought from his mind.

Talking or thinking about that day would not change the outcome. No matter what his sisters believed, analyzing his mother's death was not productive.

His thoughts now clear, he went back to the delicious meal and began asking Charlotte about her day. Abigail fed Paloma pieces of pasta in between her own bites. The meal went by too fast.

When they had finished the lasagna, Abigail put her baby girl on the blankets and started clearing the table. "Now, what we've all been waiting for! The pecan-honey pastries." She placed them on one of the fancy dishes he never used, and they all tucked into the sweet treat. Afterward, Hudson turned to Charlotte. "It's way past time to brush your teeth and get into your pajamas."

She started to protest. He held up a finger and narrowed his eyes. "We will be sleeping in your tent to-night, but no arguing. Or it's all going to be put up and you can sleep in your bed."

"Okay." Charlotte turned from him to Abigail. "Will you stay and sleep over with us?"

"No." Her response was fast and saved him from being the bad guy, something he really appreciated to-night. "I have to get Paloma home to her crib. But we'll see each other again soon. I think you've become her favorite person."

"She's mine. You won't leave without saying good-bye, will you?"

"Nope. Never." Abigail laid her palm flat against her heart. "I promise never to leave without saying good-bye."

"Enough stalling." Hudson chuckled. "Go get ready for bed. You can tell Abigail and Paloma good-night when you're done."

"All right, Daddy." She jumped off her chair and darted to the bathroom.

Hudson rose from his chair. "I'd better go check on her. You sit and relax. When I come back, we can fin-ish the dishes."

In the bathroom, he found Charlotte peering under the sink. "What are you doing?"

"Making sure nothing bad is hiding." She stood on her pink step stool and gathered her brush and tooth-paste. He pulled her hair up and braided it.

"Daddy, please let Abigail and Paloma stay the night. She could live with us, and I would have a baby sister and she could make lasagna for you every night. That would be fun."

He sighed and lowered his head so they were making eye contact in the mirror. "Charlotte. They cannot move in with us. Abigail is nice, but she is not a permanent part of our lives. She works at the bakery and is focused on her daughter. They might be our friends, but soon they'll leave town. It's just you and me, sweetheart, and that's how it's going to be until you grow up and move away. If you need anything, I will take care of it."

"I'm never going to leave you, Daddy."

He laughed, then kissed her tightly braided hair. "One day you will, and that's okay. My job is to raise you so you're ready when you want to go. Now, stop stalling and brush your teeth. After you get your pj's on, meet us at the fort."

"Okay, Daddy. I'm going to find Prancer." She turned with a huge smile. "A floppy pony is safe for a baby. Paloma will love her."

Entering the kitchen, he found Abigail washing the dishes. He took the clean plates, dried them and then put them away. This felt too right. Working together in the kitchen after a family meal had become a sad, forgotten fantasy when he'd married Zoe.

Shaking his head, he squelched the unwelcome feeling. That was treacherous territory for him and his daughter. There was no point in longing for a life that he couldn't have—not at the risk of Charlotte's trusting heart.

Apparently, he needed to have the same talk with himself that he had just had with his little girl. Clear limits needed to be set, for all their sakes.

He wasn't going to put Charlotte through the heartbreak his sisters had endured after the death of their mother.

Exhaling slowly, he put the last pot away and turned

to look at the woman who had taken over his home and head tonight. She was arranging the fruit he had in a bowl.

Abigail was an unsolved puzzle. All the warm home and hearth feelings were an illusion.

She turned and found him staring at her. With a tentative smile, she leaned back on the counter but didn't break eye contact. Silence lingered, and she seemed fine with it. Most people would want to start filling the air with words. Just letting them talk was the best way to find out what people really wanted.

But Abigail just blinked and waited for him. He cleared his throat. Why was he nervous? "First, I want to thank you for giving up your evening and making sure Charlotte was safe. Being the sheriff's daughter is not easy."

"It's not a problem. She's a sweet girl. Besides, everyone's been helping me, so it was good to be able to return the favor. Being needed every once in a while, is nice."

Moving to the living room, she checked on Paloma, then turned to look at him. "I know you're not sure if you can trust me, but I'm not going to do anything to hurt your daughter. I promise."

"You might not mean to. But I think we're on dangerous ground." He looked to the window. "A few people in town seem to want to put us together." Cutting his gaze back to her, he tried a smile. "You might have noticed. And this—" he waved a hand between them "—probably won't be the last time. But I need you to know where I stand. I'm not going to ever be interested in a romantic relationship while my daughter lives with me."

She stiffened, then lifted her chin. "Good. I've tried

playing the damsel waiting for my Prince Charming. It never worked out. I'm over the fairy tale. I'm not looking for any sort of relationship either."

Great. He'd offended her. "It's not personal. I have a feeling we're going to find ourselves thrown together in the coming weeks. No matter how many situations they engineer to work us into the same space, I can't go there. I don't want to hurt your feelings or confuse you."

"I get it." Wounded pride shone in her eyes before she turned away to pick up her daughter.

With a sigh, he perched on the edge of a barstool at the end of the large island. This was not how he wanted the evening to end. "I told you that my mother died when I was a kid. My twin sisters were eight. In less than a year, my dad was dating."

"Oh. That had to be hard." She sat down at the opposite end of the island.

"I'd already been dealing with anger and guilt, but then I watched each new girlfriend bond with my sisters and then leave. My sisters would be devastated, and there was nothing I could do to make them feel better. All my anger was directed toward my father and those women who wanted to replace my mother. It was a rough few years."

"I'm so sorry, Hudson. That had to be horrible. How old were you?"

"It started when I was fourteen. The reason I'm telling you this is that I want you to understand my decision. I won't put my daughter through that type of roller-coaster ride. And she's already asking you to move in with us."

The rigidity of her spine softened, and she laid her cheek on Paloma's head. "I get that. Having the people, you love leave you with no explanation is crushing to a child. I really care about your daughter, and I'd never intentionally hurt her, but kids see the world differently. They put expectations on the adults in their lives that can't always be lived up to. I don't even know how long I'll be in town."

The sadness in her voice urged him to ask her who abandoned her as a kid. He hated that his heart twisted at the thought of her leaving, and for both their sakes, knew he needed to change the subject. "There's been something bothering me since this morning. You had another one of your extreme reactions around a De La Rosa."

He moved closer to her. Close enough to see every detail of her reaction when he asked his question. "Do you have some sort of connection with the family I should know about? Something to do with your husband?" That was his biggest fear, and the only possibility he could come up with. But he couldn't connect the dots.

In his line of work, he tended to follow his instincts, and they were screaming that she was hiding something important.

Abigail blinked, like a deer in headlights. She was panicking. He could see the figurative gears moving through her thoughts, trying to figure out the best plan of action. She was deciding how much of the truth to tell him, if any. He had her.

He stood and leaned a hip on the counter, crossed his arms and stared at her, stone-faced. Letting her know without a word that he was not letting this go until he had the truth.

Her mouth opened, then closed. Turning away from

his gaze, she went to the sink and grabbed a glass, filling it with water.

Her daughter on her hip, she took a few sips. He allowed the heavy silence to push at her.

She finally turned to him. "My husband has nothing to do with my life now or in the future. I just… It's so complicated. My *whole life* is complicated. I'm just asking for privacy. I get the message loud and clear, Sheriff. You don't want me around your daughter." She walked around the island to the table, giving him a wide berth. "I'll get Paloma's things and leave. If Margarita or Josefina asks me to step in again to help with Charlotte, I'll make sure to say no. I understand your mistrust."

"I don't think you do." This was not what he wanted. He reached out and gently touched her arm. Then waited for her to lift her gaze to his. "Charlotte is already falling for you. But we both know you'll leave—and then I'll have to try and explain why you didn't love her enough to stay." He sighed. "On top of that, I have the whole town to protect. And the De La Rosas are special to me. They've already had too much to deal with. They are finally finding happiness, and I don't want anything or anyone to mess with that."

"Meaning?" she asked tersely.

"Meaning… I protect the people I love. Tell me what's really going on with you."

She shook her head and stepped back. He forced his hand to drop, fighting the urge to tighten his grip and hold. Not to restrain her, but to make her tell him everything.

He couldn't help her if she shut him out. With a growl, he spun away from her and ran his fingers through his hair. Why was he worried about her? He had to take care of his family, and she could be a threat on so many levels.

"If you told me what's going on, maybe I could help." *Yes. It was official.* He'd lost his mind. He should be sending her packing, not offering her help.

Her eyes were bright, but she didn't cry. "I'm so sorry. Every time I think I have a new start, I manage to mess it up. I just want to help the Espinoza family. I'll keep my distance from you and the De La Rosa family. I'm not a threat."

He wanted to believe her. So badly. But could he?

Looking down, she rubbed her eyes. "I understand about your daughter, and I respect that. Children haven't learned to guard their hearts." She sighed and picked up her sleepy baby. "As soon as she comes in, I'll say goodbye like I promised."

This was what he wanted, so why did he want to apologize? Lips pressed tight so he wouldn't say anything, he stuffed his hands into his pockets and let her gather Paloma's things.

"I found Prancer. We're ready to camp in our fort!" Charlotte entered the room waving the stuffed pony above her head.

Abigail went down on her knees. "I love your rabbit pj's and this pretty pony. You have sweet dreams tonight. Paloma and I are going."

His daughter gave a pout that rivaled her mother's.

"Charlotte. No sulking. Say goodbye," Hudson warned.

"But I have Prancer. I'll put her in the baby's bag. Oh, her bag's in my room! I'll get it for you."

"Thank you, Charlotte."

Standing, Abigail hugged Paloma close and avoided any eye contact with him.

His daughter ran from the room and was back in a few seconds. "I have it." She lifted the pink-and-green backpack trying to stuff the toy inside, then tripped on the strap. Hudson jumped to catch her, but the bag went flying into the middle of the fort, its contents scattering.

"Charlotte." Abigail rushed over to them. "Are you okay?"

"I'm sorry I spilled your stuff."

"Don't worry about that. I should have had it zipped. I just wanted to make sure you didn't get hurt."

"Nope, I'm good. Thanks for catching me, Daddy." She moved out of his arms and started hunting down all the misplaced items. Abigail joined her.

Charlotte picked up a photo. "Who are these people?"

Abigail froze mid-movement, the package of wipes in her hand forgotten.

Hudson moved to look at the picture and frowned. It showed a teenage Xavier with his brother and cousins. There was a smaller, dark-haired girl on his shoulders. He had seen the picture before. Taking the photo from Charlotte, he flipped it over. A date and each name were printed in a faded, feminine hand. "Gabby, eight years old," was the last name on the list.

He lifted his eyes to Abigail's. "Why do you have a picture of Gabby De La Rosa with her family?" A flash of anger heated him from the inside out. Had she been playing them all? Did she have plans to blackmail Xavier and his family—or worse?

Her eyes went wide, then narrowed. "How do you know Gabby?"

"Xavier is my friend. He's been looking for his sister. What do you know about her?"

"They're looking for her? For how long?"

What did she know?

"For a while. They started again when their father died." He studied her. What was safe to say? He twisted his mouth to the side, thinking, studying her. "Her aunt basically kidnapped he—"

"*What?* Kidnapped? No. Is that what they told Xavier?" Her eyes were wide and frantic.

"They?" What was she doing with this picture? Until she gave him answers, he wasn't going to tell her anything more.

"She didn't kidnap me. Belle and Elijah gave me to her."

He froze. Not possible. "Are you saying you're Gabby De La Rosa?"

She blinked. Tears slipped down her cheeks.

"Abigail?" His daughter went to her and hugged her as tightly as she could. "Please don't cry. Daddy, stop yelling at her. I don't understand. Who was kidnapped?"

Right. His daughter was in the room and confused. What was he saying? He was confused too.

Abigail wiped her face and smiled at Charlotte. "I'm okay. I just seem to be crying a lot lately. I need to get Paloma home."

She took the picture from him and stuffed a few other things into the bag. But didn't seem to care that she was leaving half her items. "Thank you for the wonderful dinner. You have a good night." She hugged Charlotte and went straight for the door.

Stopping on the threshold, she turned back and finally looked at him. "Please don't say anything to the

De La Rosas." She looked down. "I need to…" She glanced at Charlotte, then back at him. "We'll talk tomorrow?"

"Yes. I'll see you in the morning after I drop Charlotte off at school."

With a nod, she smiled at his little girl. "Thank you for the wonderful night. I had so much fun. You have a great dad. Goodbye."

"Thank you for being with me. Next time we can have a sleepover."

With a sad smile, Abigail closed the door.

Hudson helped Charlotte straighten the fort, but the whole time his mind was dealing with the fact that Abigail was the long-lost sister of his best friend. Abigail was the missing Gabby De La Rosa. Or *was* she?

Were they being played? He wanted to call Xavier, but she had asked him to wait until they talked. The De La Rosa family had waited years to get their little sister back. They could wait one more day. Depending on what she told him, maybe they would be better off not knowing her.

He knew. Hudson knew who her family was. She hadn't even had time to process it before she pulled into her parking spot.

I protect the people I love. His words played on repeat. She would never be the one he protected. But then she remembered what he'd told her about her family. Had they really been looking for her? Why did he use the word *kidnapped*? Had Belle lied to Xavier?

Paloma was asleep in the back of the car. He was going to make her tell them. Or he might tell them himself. She texted him. Please talk to me first before saying anything to anyone.

His reply was short. Yes. Provided we talk tomorrow. What if what he'd told her was all for show and they hadn't really wanted to find her? Would they even care she was in town?

Hudson didn't know the real story. Her aunt had not taken her from them. Belle and Elijah had stuffed some clothes in her backpack and told her goodbye. Her father and brothers hadn't been there. Did they even know what had happened to her? Or had they been part of it?

Could she trust any of them? Her great-aunt's words bombarded her mind. *The De La Rosa family is nothing but trouble.*

Abigail closed her eyes and searched her memories. She recalled seeing her father at the funeral, and that she'd been scared, but she couldn't remember why.

Then Belle had taken her to the room they shared and packed some of her clothes. She had been confused about what was going on. Afterward, Belle took her outside, where they had met Elijah. They each told her that it would be a short visit and that they would get her when things were settled. All she'd understood was that her mom was gone and now her family were sending her away.

She had cried and begged to stay. She had asked for her father. But her mother's aunt had pulled her off Elijah and put her into her car, then sped away. Abigail had twisted around in the seat belt and watched her cousins get smaller through the rear windshield. Where had her father and brothers been? Belle and Elijah had just stood there and let their great-aunt take her. That was the last time she had seen them or talked to them. Nothing since then. Had her cousins lied to the rest of her family?

With a sleeping Paloma tucked against her shoulder, she made her way upstairs to their cozy apartment. But it wasn't really theirs. How much longer would she be able to live off the charity of the Espinoza sisters? They had a business to run and their own families to take care of.

Tonight, she'd put the final changes she wanted to make on their website, then show it to them. Hopefully, they would see how it would make the daily running of the bakery smoother.

Going over to the crib, she gently placed her daughter inside and gazed down at her. She ran her hands over the railing that Hudson had put together for Paloma.

He was a good father. Had her dad been too? Had he wanted to keep her, but the others had sent her away? As more memories of herself as a little girl slipped through, she only grew more confused.

And then there was the horrible twist in her gut from losing Hudson. She had never had him, so why did the thought of not having him in her life upset her? He was right to be focused on his daughter.

She ran a finger along her sweet baby's cheek. "I promise to always love you above all others." She hadn't realized until tonight that her dream of a traditional family still burned under the debris of her other broken ambitions.

Cooking dinner, waiting for Hudson to come home, then sitting at the table talking about the day. For a brief moment, she felt herself fantasizing that a man would make her life perfect.

God, please heal my heart and open it to finding

peace with just my daughter. All I need to create joy in our lives is You.

She needed to write that down somewhere to remind herself in moments of weakness. Happiness like tonight was fleeting—and it might be all over with, anyway. Once everyone found out she had been lying to them, they would turn away from her.

It was what she was used to. She opened the laptop to work on the changes to the website.

She wouldn't be sleeping tonight anyway. The Bible told her not to worry, but that was the hardest habit to break.

Chapter Ten

Hudson's usually cheerful daughter was mad at him this morning. She had asked to go to the bakery before school, but he had kept making excuses until it was too late.

She'd wanted to see Abigail, but he couldn't let that happen. His daughter had started yearning for something Abigail couldn't give her.

He glanced at himself in the rearview mirror. Yeah, it wasn't just Charlotte who was drawn to the new girl in town. At the end of his disastrous marriage, he'd vowed not to bring women into their lives. Children needed stability and people they could trust.

Over the years, that promise had been easy to keep. No matter how many wonderful ladies the good folks of Port Del Mar paraded in front of him, not a single one had caused him to question his decision.

Until Abigail. Leave it to him to break his rule with a woman who came with more than a trainload of baggage and secrets. She had the power to break all of their hearts.

Hudson ran a weary hand across his face. His stomach was in knots, and he hadn't slept. He still couldn't wrap his brain around the fact she was claiming to be the missing Gabby De La Rosa.

Was she Gabby? The cynical part of his brain wondered if this was a con.

But she had to know that a simple DNA test could prove her a liar. Unless she was hoping to get the family to trust her and then tell them. But then why all the secrecy? Wouldn't she have been better off going to them first instead of hiding in town pretending to be someone else?

The parking lot in front of the bakery was full, so he pulled into a slot along the boardwalk and crossed the street. The morning crowd had taken just about every table. Usually, their weather was mild enough for the outside tables to be used, but the bizarre temperature drop had everyone huddled inside.

The bell above the door greeted him.

"Hey there, Sheriff. Close that door. It's colder than a frosted frog, and your lettin' 'em in," Grandpa Diaz hollered at him. The old man's family had lived here before the port was established, and, at ninety-five, Grandpa was one of the oldest members of the community.

"Hear a bad front's rollin' in tonight," another old-timer yelled at him.

Grandpa Diaz's great-granddaughter, Dawn, sat between the two men by the front window. It was a morning routine for them.

"They're predicting ice and snow. Is that true, Sheriff Menchaca?" the young woman asked, excitement shining in her eyes.

The old-timer cupped his mug in gnarled hands and laughed. "There ain't ever been snow in this neck of the woods. In 1983, it got so cold the bay froze. My boat was stuck right in the ice.. Wildest thing I've ever seen. But never no snow. Those fancy weather guys just like getting people all riled up."

Hudson smiled. "That's true. But even so, we're watching the reports. It would be a good night for everyone to stay home. Even if we don't get snow, patches of ice on the overpasses can cause trouble. So order a few extra pastries and hunker down for the night."

Walking up to the counter, he gave Margarita his order, then went over to Abigail at the register. She avoided eye contact while he waited.

Margarita, on the other hand, was full of good cheer. "So, how was your evening? Abigail said she had dinner with you."

"With Charlotte and Paloma," she clarified. "I told her we all had dinner."

"Oh, that's so nice. Family dinners at the end of a long day are my favorites." Margarita subtly nudged Abigail. "Charlotte likes Abigail and the baby so much. I think Abigail watching her for you is the perfect solution while Mrs. Johnson is out of town."

He was proud of his self-discipline when he didn't roll his eyes and sigh. "My sisters are coming in today."

Margarita's face fell. It was almost comical. She leaned forward to pass him his coffee and empanada. "But they have jobs. Mrs. Johnson could be gone for weeks or months."

"They work at our dad's company. Most of their work can be done from a computer, and they plan to take turns going into the office. We're not that far from Houston." He shrugged. "I think it will be nice for them to spend more time with Charlotte. They *are* her aunts."

Why was this weird guilt making him overexplain? He clamped his lips together to stop talking.

"Of course. Family's always good." Her smile was that of a woman trying to rethink her strategy. He could take advantage of that right now.

"I'd like to speak with Mrs. Dixon alone for a bit. Is that possible?"

"*Sí. Sí.* Of course." Her real smile returned, and she waved them to the back door. "I'll keep an eye on Paloma for you."

"No need. I'll take her." Abigail moved quickly to pick up her daughter, who was stacking blocks and knocking them over. "She needs to eat and have a diaper change. But thank you, Margarita."

He followed her up to the apartment. Her gaze carried a tinge of unease as it darted to him, then back to Paloma. She talked to her daughter as she pushed the stiff door open.

She turned to him. "I really do need to change her. Can you give me a moment?"

"Sure. I'm going down to get some tools out of my truck. I want to fix your door."

"My door?"

"Yes. It's hard to open."

"Okay." Her brow wrinkled in confusion.

It didn't take him long to get back up the stairs. Kneeling at the open door, he removed the old screws and replaced them with the longer ones he had purchased.

"Fixing doors. Is that a sheriff's usual job?"

"Nope. But I like things to work properly, and if you need to get into the house quickly with Paloma, struggling to open the door could waste precious moments. It's an easy fix, anyway."

He stood and tested the door. "There. Now you'll be able to get in and out without a problem."

"Thank you."

She had put Paloma in the high chair. He slid into the chair across from them as she cut up a banana.

She sighed, then looked at him. "You have a million questions. Do you doubt I'm Xavier's little sister?"

"I do have questions." He sighed. "It doesn't make sense. Why hide?"

She stiffened and focused on Paloma.

Hudson wanted to demand answers to the questions that had been circling his brain, but he knew that anything that felt like an attack would have her building walls. He needed her to open up, so he started over. "How about you tell me what you remember. You said they sent you away. Do you know when or why?"

"Apparently my mother had cancer. No one told me. I just knew she was in bed a lot. She started getting tired, that's what she told me. I would go and lie in her bed. Every day she'd read a story to me about a mother promising to always love her son, even when he got older. Then, at the end, the mother is old, maybe dying, and the son holds her.

"It made her cry, but she said the tears were her love for me. There was so much that it had to leak out. She gave me a tiny little bottle. She said she put her tears inside so that I would always have her love with me."

His chest tightened, threating to crush his lungs. What would he do if he knew he was dying and had to leave Charlotte? "She was preparing you for her death."

She nodded and wiped at her face. "I don't know

what happened to the book or the bottle. Late in March, one day after school, I went into her room and she wasn't there. Xavier was sitting on her bed. He said she had gone to heaven."

For a few minutes, she focused on her daughter. "It had to be hard for her. I can't imagine what I would do in her place." Setting the last of the banana on the tray, Abigail caressed her baby's soft curls. "I used to be angry that no one told me. But I get it now."

He nodded. "She wanted your time to be untarnished."

"That's what I think too. The day of her funeral, while we were getting dressed in our room, Belle packed a backpack. I didn't understand." She swallowed. "I didn't tell her about the bottle or book because I didn't know I was leaving."

"They sent you away on the day they buried your mother?" Anger flared, and he had to remember that Xavier and Belle were just teens at the time.

She nodded. Standing, she filled a sippy cup with water and gave it to Paloma, then lifted her out of the high chair. "My mother's aunt was at the funeral. I had never met her before. My mother's family cut off communication during her marriage to my dad. They didn't get along. My great-aunt told me stories that didn't make sense. She hated my father and anything to do with the De La Rosa family."

So Abigail had had years of being turned against her family. Things were making sense now. "She came to the funeral and took you away?"

With Paloma in her lap, she played peek-a-boo for a moment, then sat her daughter on the floor to let her explore. She sighed. "As a family, we all got into a black limousine. It seemed so big to me. We each put a flower on the coffin. I wanted to keep mine, but Daddy took it from me. We left the cemetery and went to the church's fellowship hall. My father was so sad. None of them were talking.

"Everyone else was, though. People were giving me cookies and telling how sorry they were, but that my mom was in a better place now. I wanted to go too if it was a better place." She gave him a lopsided smile. "I don't think I really understood she was gone forever."

He hated the helplessness that was squeezing his insides. That little girl needed people to hold her and love her. Hudson had felt so lost at his mother's funeral. He had also been angry and had probably snarled at anyone that got close. Especially his father. That whole month had been a blur, except for the feeling of being alone. "What happened at the church?"

"Belle and Elijah—he's my other cousin—"

"Yeah. I know who he is."

"Right. You know them better than I do." She took a deep breath. "Anyway, after the funeral they took me out past the church playground to the back parking lot. She was there, waiting next to this big black SUV. Elijah handed her my backpack."

"Just Belle and Elijah were with you?"

She turned away and blinked several times. "Yeah. I don't know where my father or brothers were."

She looked back over at him, confusion filling her gaze. "I don't know if they knew what was happening. Belle leaned down and hugged me and said it was just for now. She said they would come get me when it was safe."

"Safe?"

"Yeah. That's what she said." Her bottom lip twisted. "Then my aunt took my arm and said it was time to go. I was so scared. I lunged for Elijah, and he put his arm around me."

She moved back into the corner of the couch and pulled a pillow into her lap. "I begged him to save me. I think I yelled for Xavier and my dad. I didn't know this woman and she was taking me from my family."

They sat in silence for a bit. "I wanted to stay with them. Mamma was gone and they were all I had left. I pleaded with them not to let her take me away. But Elijah didn't say anything. He didn't *do* anything. He wouldn't even look at me. Belle was crying, but she didn't do anything either. I was put in the back seat and that was it. I called out to them, still begging, but they didn't move. I twisted around to see if they were going to come after me. They stood there until I couldn't see them anymore."

The room went silent. She was lost in that little girl's trauma. She had to be Gabby. Either that, or she was the best actress he'd ever seen. There was no reason not to believe her version. It was missing the pieces that would help her make sense of the reasons why they'd sent her away. They had thought they were protecting her. But it had left a little girl lost and confused.

He went to the couch and sat next to her, wishing he could hold that traumatized little girl. Taking Abigail's hand, he gently squeezed it. "What do you remember about your father?"

She shook her head. "I remember he was tall—but back then I was small, so I'm not sure that's reliable." She pulled her hand out of his and twisted her fingers. "He would take me riding on his horse. He taught me how to sit in the saddle and use the reins. There were times when we played games in the kitchen—chutes and ladders, Candyland and card games."

"Those are good memories."

Turning in her seat, she watched Paloma scoot around the coffee table, picking up toys and chewing on them. "They seem incomplete. Since I've been back in town, there seem to be memories behind a fog. I can't clear it away."

He wanted to ask her if she was ever afraid of her dad, or if he was ever violent—but those were leading questions. He wanted to know what she remembered. "Do you remember him with your cousins, your brothers?"

Wrapping her arms around her middle, she pulled into herself. Her eyes searched the room as if she would find the answers somewhere in the apartment. "Why was it only Belle and Elijah that took me to my aunt? Did my dad and my brothers know?"

Hudson rubbed his temples. He wasn't sure how to handle all this. Xavier had told him that their father was a violent drunk that abused the older kids. This was his friend's tale to tell. But there were so many gaps Abigail needed filled.

"Xavier talked to me. He and Damian knew they were taking you to your aunt. It had been set up before your mother's death. From what I understand, they had asked her to take you temporarily. Abigail, your father was a violent man. When they reached out your aunt cut them off. Then she moved and they couldn't find you."

Her head shook in denial. "That doesn't make any sense. I don't remember my father being violent. And we did move a couple of times, but we should have been easy to find." Abigail looked so lost and alone. Hudson moved closer and put his arm around her. She closed her eyes and leaned into him.

"She changed your name. Changed her phone. Mail was sent back. She went into hiding with you. From what I understand, she thought your father was dangerous and she didn't trust your brothers."

Curled up against him, she was quiet for a long time. Paloma's babbling was the only sound in the room. "She did change my name. I never knew the ranch's number or address."

She sighed. "When I was little, Daddy was gone a lot. I always thought he was working. But when he was home, I remember the nights we had dinner together. He would tell us stories about the ranch and his dad and granddad. I wanted to be his cowgirl and work the ranch by his side. None of this is making sense. There were nights when Belle would pull me into her bed and wrap us under her blanket, holding me while a loud storm passed over the house. She said it was a storm, but there was never any rain."

She pulled her knees up and worried her bottom lip. "You said that you and Xavier are good friends. You're not from here, so where did you meet him?"

"Military. Xavier joined to get away from his father. We served together. Abigail, your father had some troubling issues when he drank. From what I know, your brothers and cousins were trying to protect you."

She took a deep breath in and laid her head against his shoulder. "My mom raised my cousins. Did you know that? Their mother left them. My childhood memories are so messed up. There were nights that Belle didn't come to our room. When I asked her where she went, she said a friend's. But we weren't allowed to go to anyone's house. Did Xavier tell you where she was? Did it have to do with my father?"

"He said there was a shed, and when he was mad at them for not doing something right, they would have to stay in the shed. Your mother would keep things from getting too violent, but when she got sick, he started using the shed more. With her gone, it got worse. Xavier told me your father went into a rage after your mother died and they were all worried that they couldn't protect you. He was unpredictable. Sending you to stay with your aunt for a few months or a year was the best option. They tried to call you but she wouldn't let them talk to you. When they went to the house, you'd moved. They tried to find you. When they finally found your aunt, she told them that you'd run away, and she didn't know where you were."

"That's not true," she protested. "When I was seventeen, she kicked me out. I stayed with friends until I went to college. I stayed in contact with her the whole time."

"She lied to you and them. You need to tell your brothers who you are."

"I don't know. It's so much to take in." She released a quavering breath. "I don't know what to think. I came here with the idea of finding my dad. And I thought if I could find him, then everything would be okay. But he's gone. I don't know who to trust."

"Abigail, they've been looking for Gabby. You need to let them know that you're here in town and that you're okay."

She shook her head. "If they'd really wanted to find

me, I think they could have. How do you know their version of the story is true?"

Jaw clenched, he tilted his head back and looked at the ceiling. "They're your family. You might feel like you've been abandoned by them, but I believe Xavier when he said they did the best they could at the time. They were teenagers who had just lost their mom and were scared of their dad. Was it right to sneak you off that way? No. But now you have an opportunity to connect with your family, and you should take it."

Great. Now he was a hypocrite. When was the last time he'd had a real conversation with his father? He hadn't even invited him to his home here in Port Del Mar. But that situation was different, right?

His hand stroked Abigail's upper arm and back. Yeah, they were a mess. But she didn't know what a gift her family would be. The De La Rosas were good people.

Just like his dad. His head fell back against the sofa, and he stared at the ceiling. He was so tired of being angry about something he had no control over. Did his father still hate him?

Shifting, he laid his cheek against her forehead. "You're here in your hometown for a reason. The Espinozas have been great, but they are not your family. Don't miss this opportunity and waste any more time."

She leaned into him. He wasn't sure who was getting more comfort from the contact. They lingered like that for a moment then she gently pulled away from him.

The space between them left him cold. At the opposite end of the sofa, she tucked her legs underneath her. "There are families you are born into, then there are families you make. I've decided to make my family. If they'll let me, I want to make the Espinozas my family. I don't know the De La Rosas." She lifted her chin. "I came to town to find my dad, and he's dead. I don't know if I want to meet the cousins and the brothers who sent me away. They don't have anything that I need."

He took a deep breath. She was being stubborn. Hurt and pride had a way of doing that to a person. He should know.

Chewing on the inside of his mouth, he studied her for a moment. "I want to tell you something I've never told anyone—not even my family or my ex-wife."

His chest burned at the thought of telling this story, but she opened up a painful memory for him. Maybe this would help her.

"The day my mother was shot." His throat burned. A few deep breaths and he tried again. "That day, she hadn't wanted to stop at the convenience store. But I complained and whined that I was hungry and thirsty, so she finally took me in. While I was grabbing a drink, a man came in. I hadn't even realized what was happening when my mother knocked me to the ground."

Abigail moved back over to him and pressed a warm hand against his rapidly beating heart. "Hudson, you don't have to—"

He touched his fingertips against her mouth. "Let me tell the story." He felt hollow on the inside. A giant cavern opened. "She covered me, telling me she loved me and that it would be okay. The rest was a blur."

His throat had gone dry. Taking a moment to collect himself, he looked at his hands. "Literally nothing but motion, sounds and people screaming, then a weird silence."

He had to pause. "I didn't understand what was going

on. I felt warmth and blood. We just lay there, me with my arms around my mom. Her breathing became really labored. I don't remember how long we were like that. Someone with a uniform—maybe an EMT—took her off me. She went into an ambulance. I was taken to the hospital in the back of a police car."

The emptiness and confusion were back. This was why he never thought about this day. It was too hard. "I was alone in a room for what seemed like forever— I think people talked to me and offered me food, but I don't remember anything until my dad came in. He's the one who told me she was gone."

Abigail had moved into his arms, and he pulled her close. Holding her the way he wished he could hold on to his mom, he clung to her.

"I never told my dad that it was my fault." The words came out hoarsely; his throat was raw. "It was my fault that my mom, *his wife*, was dead. It was one moment that changed our lives. Me not wanting to wait for dinner. I don't see how he could ever forgive me. We don't even really talk anymore. It's too painful."

"Hudson. You can't—"

"Shh. Time with your family is precious. I know I have a heightened sense of protecting others. I've made it my job. But the list of people I let in is very short. I have to keep it manageable."

He took a deep breath and moved back. "Xavier, Damian, Belle and Elijah need to be given a chance to love you. You might not need them, but they need to know that you're okay. Please tell me that you'll go to them by the end of the week."

He pulled her back into his arms. Yeah, he liked to keep his list of people he cared about short. But he had a feeling that, no matter what he told himself, the distance he kept or how professional he tried to be, it was too late. He cared very deeply for Abigail and her daughter. They had made his short list.

"What if you have it wrong and they don't want me on the ranch? That I'm just another complication they would rather do without."

Leaning in and pressing his cheek to the side of her head, he whispered, "What if they love you more than you imagined and you coming home is a dream come true for them? If you hide and never ask, you'll never know."

Hope was the most dangerous thing he could give her. "If I give in to that hope, I give my family the power to destroy me when they shut the door on us."

The mental image of her standing alone on the old porch with Paloma in her arms was so vivid. The sound of a door slamming shut echoed in her brain. Her mother's bedroom door. The way her aunt had kicked her out. How the police had slammed the door when her husband had been arrested. She had been left standing alone each time. No goodbyes.

"You have proven how resilient you are. Put your hope and faith in God. But give your family the opportunity to bring you in."

"I'm so tired of being resilient." That was a level of hope that would crush her if she let it steal into her heart. If they didn't want her, she would have to leave Port Del Mar. What she couldn't speak out loud was her biggest fear.

But it was pointless to hide the truth from herself. It wasn't her family's rejection that scared her the most; it was Hudson's. He had made it clear there was no room for her in his life.

This wonderful, generous man had been hurt by his family and his wife. He wasn't going to risk his heart on her, and that made him very dangerous. Falling in love with him would be so easy to do—and would fit right into her pattern of self-destructive behaviors.

After all the hurts and disappointments she had lived through, she knew better than to rely on anyone for security. On one hand, Hudson could be her lifeline in this storm. On the other, he could be the boat that sank her.

All she wanted was peace, happiness and family. Why was that so difficult for her to attain? What had she done wrong? What plans did God have in store for her?

Paloma banged a cup on the coffee table and yelled. Laughing, Abigail moved away from Hudson's warmth and sat on the floor next to her daughter. "Someone wants my attention. What is it? You want more? You have to ask nicely. Please."

Hudson stood. "It's time for me to head out. When are you going to tell them?"

He was so tall that she had to bend her neck to a ninety-degree angle to look up at him. "I didn't say I was going to tell them. Are you trying to intimidate me?"

With a sigh, he dropped to his haunches. "No."

Paloma handed him her cup and babbled some noises. "You want more water?" His large hand swallowed up her cup. Standing, he went to the kitchen and refilled it.

Her stupid, lonely heart wanted her to notice how terrific he was as a father. It didn't matter that he didn't want them on his short list.

Handing the cup to her daughter, he looked at her. "When are you going to tell them?" he repeated.

"Give me a week." She stood and picked up Paloma. "I want to think about how I'm going to do it. What I want to say. Maybe I'll write a letter."

"You say, 'Hi, I'm Gabby. I'm in town and would love to get to know you.'"

She rolled her eyes, then shook her head. "If it's so easy, when are you calling your dad?"

He narrowed his eyes, but before he could say anything, his phone went off. Glancing at it, he smiled. "It's my sisters. They're downstairs." He put a finger out for Paloma to grab. "Want to meet the two smartest, silliest, pain-in-my-neck women?"

Abigail had overheard a few phone conversations with his sisters, and Charlotte had gone on about how wonderful and funny her aunts were. Theirs was the kind of relationship she dreamed of having with her siblings.

"Are you coming down?" His piercing gaze held her in place and brought her back to the moment.

"Yes. Let me get Paloma's bag." She sat her daughter down on the sofa and went to get the backpack out of her room.

If she was honest with herself, she was disappointed that he'd called his sisters in instead of asking her to watch Charlotte. But he was careful about the people he allowed into his daughter's life. It was the right thing to do. She would have doubts letting someone with her baggage watch her daughter.

She was feeling raw and vulnerable because of the deep family secrets they had shared today. Yet each time Hudson was around, she felt safe and comforted to have him close.

That worried her. There was no way she could allow herself to become dependent on him.

Coming back into the living room, she found him texting on his phone. "Everything okay?"

Looking up, he nodded. "I told my sisters that you were coming down to meet them and they screamed like teenagers at a concert. Apparently, they've been wanting an introduction for a while. Someone has told them all about you. Or should I say *several* someones have."

"Me? What are people telling them about me?" She brushed past him to reach Paloma and had to stop. The coffee table was in the way. He leaned into her as she looked up.

They froze for a second. His eyes went to her lips. Was he going to kiss her? Her lungs stopped working. The woodsy smell of him surrounded her. Inviting her to risk her heart.

He stepped back and cleared his throat. "Sorry. Didn't mean to get in your way."

She nodded and smiled. "Oh no. It's okay." But it wasn't anywhere close to being okay. It would be so easy to fall for him. But no one had to warn her how it would end. She knew. He'd leave her. Like everyone else.

Paloma on her hip, she followed him to the shop. As soon as they stepped inside there were identical women standing on each side of her.

"This must be Paloma, the amazing little girl we've heard all about." They looked from the baby to her. "Hello. I'm Madison and this is Liberty."

They were softer and a little bit lighter in coloring than Hudson, but she could see the family resemblance.

"Hi. I'm Abigail."

"We know." With a smile to light up the Texas Stadium, Liberty patted her arm. She cut a glance to Margarita and Josefina at the counter. "They have kept us updated on you and our brother. Which is good because he never tells us anything important. But we do have to check out things for ourselves you know. Someone has to protect our big brother."

"So, tell us everything about you and your plans," the other twin picked up.

Abigail blinked. "Updates?"

Hudson's sigh was so deep she could feel it. He took her free hand and pulled her away from the twins.

"How about you give her some space so we can sit down? I'll tell you everything you need to know. Not that there is anything to know." He cut a glare to the sisters behind them. And it sounded like he muttered traitors under his breath.

His sisters laughed and followed to the corner table in the back.

Liberty reached for Paloma. "Can I hold her please. I'm sure you have seen what a great father Hudson is."

"Liberty." Hudson just about growled his sister's name. She laughed and took the baby.

"How about we start with stories about Hudson as a boy. Then you can share." The sisters went on to tell her amusing stories of their childhood.

Hudson rolled his eyes, but he didn't hide the smile the memories brought.

Shared memories were a blessing of family. They

knew all the weakness and ugly spots. They also knew the joys and greatest moments.

This was what her heart longed for with her brothers and cousins.

In reality some people never had this. She feared she was going to one of those.

Chapter Eleven

Abigail leaned forward to check her hair. It had been a couple months now without a trim. It was still short, but the severe edge had softened. Tilting her head, she studied how the light reflected in the new color she added last night. She had tried to return it to her natural color, but it had been so long since she started bleaching it, she wasn't sure. She looked like a stranger.

Resa bumped her shoulder and smiled. "You look great. But if we don't join the family soon, Mamma will come looking for us, and that's not good. We need to be seated before the first song starts."

Now that she was going to church with the Espinoza family, she had gained a new peace. She had a church family. Of course, it being a small town, Hudson and the De La Rosas also attended the same church.

For the first time in her life, she felt as though she had real friends and family. She had shown Margarita and Josefina the website and they were so excited about things they had never even thought about before. It had gone live, and orders and payments had increased.

As she followed Resa to the Espinoza pews, people

smiled at them. Margarita had explained that the pews didn't really belong to anyone, but after so many generations, families had their spaces. And some of the old-timers got downright territorial.

Abigail loved it. She glanced over to the right side a little farther up. That's where her brothers and cousins sat with their families. Her gut twisted. She hadn't come up with a plan yet, but she ran out of time. Hudson would not hesitate to tell them if he thought she was going to keep hiding.

During her devotional on Wednesday, she'd had an epiphany. Saying she had turned everything over to God was not the same as actually doing it. She was still struggling with trusting Him completely.

A shadow fell over her. Turning, she looked up into Hudson's indigo-and-gold eyes. He nodded to her, then indicated he wanted to sit next to her. Nerves slammed into her chest. She wasn't ready to talk to him, for him to be so close. He just stood there, waiting, as people started looking at them. Resa pulled her over to make room for him.

"Thank you." He sat down and looked straight ahead. At the front of the church was a beautiful painting of a sunrise over the ocean. Rays of light came down from heaven, and a dove formed the center of the scene. The Holy Spirit. She loved the serenity it gave her. It reminded her that God was in every part of every day, from sunup to deep in the night.

She took a deep breath and relaxed.

Hudson leaned in closer. "Charlotte saw Paloma in the nursery and wanted to stay with her."

Was he concerned that their daughters had bonded? Or did he feel the same wave of contentment that she felt whenever the girls were together? Sighing, she kept her gaze forward, focusing on the dove. The service hadn't started yet, and people were still chatting and greeting each other. He leaned in again. "You told me a week. Time is up. When are you going to tell them?"

She turned and glared at him. "Soon. I have a plan." She was working on one, anyway, but she was procrastinating. Hudson didn't need to know that. That was between her and God.

"It's only going to get harder the longer you wait. And I don't like knowing something this big and keeping it from my friends. They're good people."

Guilt hit her. She hadn't thought of how it made him feel. "I'm sorry. I promise, I'm going to do it. I just need to figure out the right time."

"What are you going to do?" Resa leaned in from her other side, a twinkle in her eye. "You two going on a date?"

"No." They both answered in a harsh whisper at the same time. People were starting to look at them.

Resa nudged her but kept looking at Hudson. "They're wondering if you're sweet on her. I mean, you are sitting with us instead of your sisters." She winked. Being in the middle of seven kids, Resa didn't think twice about teasing people and getting in their business.

The music started, and they all fell quiet. Abigail let the notes fill her and lift her heart to the heavens. In this world of uncertainty, God was the keystone.

She loved this little church. Every Sunday there was a new message that inspired her. It was as if God had a lesson ready each week just for her.

This time, the pastor talked about learning to let God's plan work in everyone's lives. He was right. Abigail knew she had to open her heart to new possibilities. Reading from the Bible and telling stories, the pastor made it sound easy. She made a note of the scriptures so that when Monday rolled around and she stumbled, the Word could pull her back onto the right path.

When the last worship song had finished, people started milling around, chatting and making lunch plans. Peace and warmth filled her.

Hudson scooted out and waited for her and Resa to join him. Abigail stood, then stepped back to let the other woman out. She glanced over at the De La Rosa family. They were in a cluster, but then Belle turned and smiled at her. All Abigail's warm, hopeful feelings froze as her cousin walked straight over to her.

"Abigail!" Belle hugged her. "It's so good to see you. I was going to go by the bakery Monday, but this saves me a trip. Well, I'll still come by for my chocolate croissant." She laughed.

Abigail didn't know what to do. Belle was standing in front of her talking like they were friends. Every muscle in her body went rigid. Her eyes darted to Hudson, and he lifted one brow and smirked at her.

She'd get no help from him. Sheriff Menchaca was enjoying this too much.

"I just had to tell you how much I love, love, love the new *panadería* website. I was told you designed and built the whole thing. It's so perfect for the bakery and so easy to use." Belle stepped back, but she kept her hand on Abigail's arm. "Anyway, it gave me some wonderful ideas."

Resa came out of the pew and joined them. "Hi, Resa," Belle greeted her. "Where are Margarita and Josefina? I wanted to talk to them too."

"They went to get the kids. We're meeting them out front," the younger Espinoza replied. "I'm heading out now. I'll see you in a bit, Abigail. Hudson, will you and your family be joining us for lunch?"

"Charlotte would be mad if I said no."

Resa squeezed his arm as she passed by. "Yeah, it's all about Charlotte." She winked at Abigail.

Heat climbed her neck. Why were people forcing her on Hudson? Poor man, he was going to start hating the sight of her.

"I was hoping we could talk about a cross-promotion." Belle was talking to her.

Good. That gave her something to focus on as she tried to ignore the man next to her.

"A cross-promotion?" She had lost track of the conversation.

"Yes. We're turning two, maybe three of our cabins on the ranch into short-term rentals. I was trying to think of ways to make it personal and homey. You had some gift basket ideas on the website." Bella's eyes lit up. "Wouldn't that be a perfect little welcome basket when someone stepped into the cabin? Sweets from the bakery along with the freshly ground coffee beans? Maybe a few things from our tackle and gift shop on the pier?" She raised her eyebrows in excitement, looking at Abigail as she waited for a response.

Abigail was still having a hard time realizing that Belle was talking to her. She managed a smile and a nod, hopefully convincing her she was listening.

Her cousin glanced at Hudson. "Have you seen the site? It makes me want to visit Port Del Mar and eat up all the goodness." She turned back to Abigail. "We could pull in other local merchants."

This was exactly what Abigail had envisioned when she had put the small gift baskets on the site. Taking a deep breath, she finally found her voice. "I have more ideas about putting together Port Del Mar baskets and using them to promote local products. It's that personal touch that brings people to a small town like this. I've been putting together some gift baskets with different themes. I can show them to you. Each season could have a different basket."

"Yes!" Belle grabbed her arm.

Now Abigail was excited too. She'd thought it would take longer to approach people about her idea. "We could also customize them if they wanted to add certain items and have them all ready when they arrive."

Belle nodded. "That sounds perfect. It's exactly what I'm thinking. Now, get the boys on board."

"The boys?"

"My brother and cousins. I run the ranch, but they have input. And they own so many local businesses, but they don't get the whole personal touches for profit. Having those small details is important to rebooking, good reviews and spreading the word. My goal is to have at least 75 percent occupancy. I think things like that are what bring people back and get them telling other people about it."

Abigail nodded. "I can bring something out to show you later today. Around six or seven?"

"That would be great! Then we wouldn't just be telling them—we can *show* them. Come out at five—the whole family will be at the ranch for dinner. We can all eat together, then hit them with the presentation."

Abigail was thinking ahead of all the different specialty shops in town she had wanted to include. "I could put three or four packages together. Some manly fishing ones and a spa-day type of basket. Really, the possibilities are endless."

Bella clapped her hands together. "Yes! Oh my gosh, I knew I loved you. That is so good—and we've got the restaurants. The fishing charters and the pier gift shop. If you need anything, let me know, or Julie, our office manager. We could really have fun with this. Let's wow the boys." Then she furrowed her brow. "Are you sure you can get something ready by tonight?"

"Yes, this is something I've already been playing around with. I have several packages sketched out."

"Sounds great! And fair warning… Sunday dinner with the De La Rosas is quite the event! There's lots of us, so it won't be a quiet affair." She looked over her shoulder as her husband, Quinn, waved at her. "The kids are getting restless. I have to go, but I'm excited to see what you bring us. Thank you, Abigail." She turned and walked off, joining her husband and their five kids.

She was going to the De La Rosa ranch.

For a moment, she couldn't breathe. She was going to go have dinner with them. Belle had invited her into their home. She wasn't going to have to show up uninvited.

Of course, they didn't know who she was.

"Stop." Hudson's voice was low but strong. "Don't overthink this invitation. It's an informal business meeting with dinner. Before you leave, ask for a few minutes alone with Belle. Start with her. Or tell the whole family at once. But you can't deny this is a perfect opportunity that has been set at your feet."

She nodded. She had just promised to have an open door to God's plan, and then Belle came over and invited her to the ranch. "It looks that way, doesn't it? My planning is done, and now it's time to do."

Hudson chuckled. "I couldn't have said it better myself. If you need anything, you have my number. To ease your nerves, I suggest you think of the best-case scenario and a worst-case one. Go in knowing you have a plan no matter what happens."

"Yes. Thank you."

"You've got this. Trust that ultimately God is in control. And bundle up. The weather is supposed to get rough tonight with temps dropping. It might get below freezing."

She had to laugh. "Really? It was sixty-five today. Plus, I've lived in Ohio for so many years. I can handle the cold."

He gave her a little salute. "Yes, ma'am."

The weather was the least of her worries. She was finally going to the ranch. After years of dreaming about it, it was happening.

"Abigail." His warm hand gently squeezed her shoulder. "It's going to be okay. You're about to find out how much your family loves you."

"Are you sure? They haven't recognized me. Even after I dyed my hair back to its natural color. What if they don't believe it's me? And then there's the whole mess with my ex…"

"Good. You're planning the worst-case scenario already. What will you do if that happens?"

She laughed. "Nice pep talk."

"That's why I'm here. But really, Abigail, it's going to be fine. And you'll be mad at yourself for waiting so long. But don't fixate on that. Shame and regret are a waste of time. Enjoy your family and know that God brought you to this point at *this time* for a reason."

"Thank you."

With a lopsided smile, he turned and walked out of the sanctuary. A few people were still meandering. Margarita stood at the front door with a group of Espinoza kids. Her oldest daughter held a smiling Paloma.

Margarita waved her over and Abigail joined them. She was going to spend some time with her favorite new family before heading out to meet her old one.

What was going to happen when they found out that the little sister, they had sent away was back in town— and had been for a while now?

She hoped Hudson was right and that they would welcome her and Paloma.

Halfway to the side door, Hudson saw his daughter. She was giggling at something his sister was saying. His heart twisted. He'd give about anything to protect her innocence. A twinge of melancholy clouded his thoughts.

Eventually, Charlotte would grow up and someone would hurt her, no matter how hard he tried to protect her. Liberty, the older of his twin sisters, poked her head around the edge of the door. There was pure glee shining in her golden eyes. He had a bad feeling it was at his expense. He glared at his sister.

She made an attempt to glare back, but she couldn't hold it for long and ended up grinning. "What are you so grim about?" she asked.

He stepped through the doorway and found his other sister, Madison, waiting behind them. They were both smiling.

"What are you so happy about?" Great, his little sisters had him resorting to his fourteen-year-old self.

Liberty put her hand on her hip and taunted him with all her sass. "Wouldn't you like to know?"

Jumping up and down, Charlotte called for his attention. "Daddy!"

"What is it, little bear?" He picked her up.

Her small hands touched his face. "Tía Liberty said that you were making a poor attempt at flirting." Her smile was so big, it took up her whole face. "Were you flirting with Ms. Abigail?"

"No. But what do you know about flirting?" Eyes narrowed, he cut a hard glare at his sister.

"It's what boys do when they want a girlfriend. Abigail would be a great girlfriend for us."

"I think your aunt has been saying very inappropriate things and needs a time-out."

Neither his tone nor his expression intimidated her. With a smirk, Liberty shrugged. "Why aren't you flirting? You're a decent enough guy. You're not old. You should be flirting."

"Yes!" Charlotte agreed. "I think you're the bestest. I would marry you, but Tía Maddy says I can't."

Hudson tilted his head back to the ceiling. *One. Two. Three.*

He loved his sisters, but they were the best at pushing his buttons. He was an adult and not here for their free entertainment. He lowered his chin and looked at Liberty. "You shouldn't be saying these kinds of things to my daughter."

She blew out a puff of air. "I know we've both told you many times and it bears repeating. You, big brother, take yourself way too seriously."

"I'm a single dad and a sheriff. They need me to be a responsible adult."

"We're just worried about you and want you to be happy. It would help if you smiled every once in a while and were nice to people," Madison said, her expression much more serious.

"I am nice to people. All the time. Unless they are breaking a law or being a pest." He gave her a pointed look. "Stop being a pest and you'll get to meet the nice me."

"Daddy is nice. And he has the best smile." His daughter looked confused by the tension between her favorite people.

He kissed her cheek and set her on the ground. "Thank you."

"I'm hungry, Daddy."

Thankful Charlotte had changed the subject, he jumped on it. "Then it's time to have some lunch. We were invited to join the Espinozas at Bridges's house. Do you want to go?"

"Yes." His daughter squealed. This was accompanied by clapping and more jumping. "And Daddy, you can practice flirting. Abigail and Paloma are going to be there."

He let out a groan before he could pull it back. His sister was laughing out loud as she went down the hall and out into the parking lot.

"What's so funny, Tía Liberty?"

"Your daddy. He thinks he's so smart."

"He is smart."

He loved that he could do no wrong in his daughter's eyes. How long would that last?

Liberty took Charlotte's hand. "Oh, he is smart. Too

smart for his own good. I think God has some plans for him that are about to shake his foundation."

"My foundation is fine, thank you very much."

"Oooh! This is going to be fun. There's a rumor going around that your single days are numbered. Wonder what they're talking about?" His sister almost danced her way to his Jeep Gladiator. "The debate in front of the feedstore this morning was about how long it'll take for you to ask her out. I guess we aren't the only ones that noticed your daddy giving Ms. Abigail goo-goo eyes."

"Goo-goo eyes?" He might have shouted. Several people in the parking lot looked over at them. Of course, his sisters were laughing so hard they doubled over.

"You're executives at a financial firm. Act like it." He took a moment to steady his breathing. He was allowing them to push his buttons again. "Never mind. Let's go home. Maybe there your *tía* Liberty and *tía* Madison can learn enough manners to go out in public."

"Please, Daddy. I want to go see Desirae, Josh and Paloma. And Angie and Nica too."

She loved hanging around Margarita and Josefina's kids as much as possible. Being an only child was tough on her.

Charlotte's eyes were big as her bottom lip puckered. It was the saddest face, but it was her eyes that got him every time. They were so much like his mom's.

Putting an arm around his daughter, he pulled her close. "I'm just being grumpy. Your aunts do that to me sometimes."

"I promise to use good manners, Daddy." She turned to look at Madison then Liberty. "You will too, right?"

"Yes. We promise to use our best manners." Liberty

spoke, but both of his sisters laid their hands over their chest, trying to act innocent.

Charlotte hugged his legs. "We'll be good, Daddy. Can we please go to the Espinozas' house for lunch?"

Hudson took a deep breath and forced his taut muscles to relax. "Fine. We'll pick up a pie and head that way. Now get in the truck."

He helped her buckle up in the back seat, then stepped out and put a hand on Liberty's door to block her. His other hand gently stopped Madison as she headed to the other side of the Jeep. He bent down to Liberty's level, going nose to nose just like when they were younger and he had to get her attention.

She was always joking and pulling pranks, while Madison would follow along. "I know you're joking and you think it's funny, but I don't want Charlotte confused. The other night she asked me to let Abigail and Paloma move in with us. She wants a sister so badly. Maybe even a mother. That's why I asked you and Madison to help me out. I can't let her get too attached to Abigail and her daughter."

Liberty blinked, moisture gathering in her eyes. "Oh, Hudson…"

"No. Don't be sad. Just stop kidding around about it. This is serious, and I don't want Charlotte hurt. You should understand that." Did she remember how much she and Madison had cried every time their dad broke it off with his latest girlfriend? His throat burned.

He had been so helpless, unable to make them feel better as they wept. "I have to take care of my daughter and protect her heart while I still can. I know you're just messing around and playing, but it can have serious consequences to a six-year-old who doesn't understand. So, stop it. Okay?"

She lifted her eyes to his, her glance so much like their mother's that his gut twisted. She touched his cheek. "We're worried about you. We miss the guy you were before Zoe tricked you into marriage, then deserted you and Charlotte."

He looked away, flexing his jaw. He hated that his ex-wife could still hurt his family. "This is not about Zoe, it's about you filling my daughter's head with ideas that won't ever materialize."

He cut his gaze to Madison.

She nodded. "We know how important she is to you. You're the best dad. But you're a person too. You're more than her father and the sheriff of this town." She took a step closer to him. "You deserve happiness too, big brother."

"I am happy." He glanced over his shoulder. His daughter was sitting in the back seat chatting to her hand. It was apparently talking back. Man, he loved that little girl. "We should go." He dropped Madison's hand and moved around Liberty.

"Hudson, I'm sorry." Liberty reached for him this time. "You know I would never do anything to hurt her or you."

He nodded as she opened her door and climbed in. By the time he walked around the front of his truck, Liberty was in the front seat and Madison was having a full-blown conversation about sea turtles with his daughter.

He was responsible for this gift God had given him. All his attention and love were hers.

Before he closed his door, he heard laughter floating across the parking lot. When he turned toward the source, he saw Abigail standing with Josefina and Noah, the youngest Espinoza. He was closer to Abigail's age.

Hudson's lungs tightened at the thought of the two of them going out on a date. Noah leaned in and whispered something, causing Abigail to throw her head back and laugh.

Josefina looked put out. He could relate. But he had zero business being any kind of jealous. If Abigail wanted to go on a date with a kid who didn't take anything seriously, well then Noah was her guy.

Charlotte asked a question and he nodded, but his mind was wrapped up in Abigail.

He knew how worried she was about telling her family who she really was. And he knew Xavier. The De La Rosas would pull her into their fold. She wouldn't need him to have her back; she'd have her family and the Espinozas. Two large families that understood loyalty and caring for others.

But then again, Xavier could also be cynical. With his history it was understandable.

If there was the slightest hesitation, Abigail would be hurt and might close down.

He should have told her he'd go with her. As he started his truck, a text came in. It was Abigail. Don't worry about Charlotte seeing me at lunch. I'm going home to get ready for tonight.

She was respecting his wishes and staying away from his daughter. He hated that that made him sad.

Chapter Twelve

Abigail leaned forward over the steering wheel. Snow flurries had started falling, but they were nothing compared to those in Ohio. As she drove, the flurries turned to huge, fluffy flakes. Then they disappeared and ice pellets pelted her windshield.

Texas had some roller-coaster weather reports. At least it was still daylight and she could see where she was going. She checked her phone. Only a couple of miles to the ranch. Glancing up at her rearview mirror, she saw that Paloma had fallen asleep.

The car slid to the right, even though she hadn't turned the wheel. She wasn't in control...they were gliding. *Ice.*

Taking her foot off the gas, she let the car coast. She knew that fighting it could make it worse. There weren't any cars on the road, so that was good.

But then her heart went into overdrive as the car veered off the road into a ditch and came to an abrupt stop. The big fat snowflakes were back, and the road looked wet with a little snow. It didn't look icy. She had hit a patch of black ice.

She twisted around to check on Paloma. She was awake and rubbing her eyes but thankfully seemed to be okay. "Looks like we're in a pickle, baby girl." And they were so close to the ranch.

"Ma. Ma. Ma," her daughter replied.

Putting the car in reverse, Abigail tried to carefully back out. That didn't work. The front grille was buried in a snow-covered dune, so there was no going forward. "We are definitely stuck." Should she call the Espinoza sisters?

Hudson would be the obvious choice, but she felt so lame. "It was just this morning I was bragging about my driving skills in winter weather." She looked at her daughter. "I could just call 911."

The dunes blocked their view of the ocean, and on the other side was flat marshy land and water. The town was ten miles behind them and the ranch was two miles ahead.

There were several blankets in the back, she should get those. She reached for the phone to call Margarita and a text came through. It popped up on her dashboard screen too.

Hudson. There was no way he was going to let her forget that a girl who'd just come from Ohio couldn't drive in Texas winter weather. Opening the door, she felt the cold wind hit her face and take her breath. Careful not to slip on the ice, she made her way to the trunk for the blankets.

She opened the text. Are you still at home?

The next one was just a minute later.

Reports are warning that bad weather is hitting us. We're closing all the country roads. Where are you?

Abigail?

She was going to have to call him and admit she had underestimated the Texas weather. She'd call Hudson as soon as she got Paloma settled and warm. Her hands were already stiff; she hadn't even brought her gloves.

With the trunk opened, she gathered the three blankets. Her phone was ringing. She couldn't see who it was, but she imagined it was Hudson since she hadn't replied to any of his texts. It stopped, then started again. "Hold your horses. I'll answer you soon as I can."

She wrapped the blanket around Paloma. She was babbling and chewing on the corner of her cloth butterfly book. The phone started chiming again. Her hands now free, she answered it this time.

"Hello." Did he hear the shaking in her voice? It was so cold.

"Abigail, are y'all okay? Where are you? The conditions are getting worse by the second. Texas weather is so unpredictable."

"We're both fine." She sighed as she put him on speaker and rubbed her hands tighter. "Well, as fine as we can be in a ditch on the side of the road."

"What happened?" She could hear the deep concern in his voice.

"I hit a patch of black ice about two miles from the ranch. I was going slow and there were no other cars around. We're okay, but I don't have enough traction to get out. It's a little embarrassing since I had just been bragging about my driving skills in winter weather."

"Nothing you can do about ice. There's no way anyone can drive on it. But you're safe and warm?"

"Yes. I have blankets in the trunk. The car doesn't seem to have any damage. Paloma is talking and reading a book."

"Hang tight. It'll take me a little longer to get there with the chains on my tires. Should be about fifteen to twenty minutes out." He hung up before she could tell him to be careful.

She turned to face her daughter. "Help is on the way. We seem to have our own cowboy who's riding in and saving the day."

The snow was coming down thicker. A blanket of white was starting to cover everything. At least Hudson should be able to see her red car. One of the things she had been most excited about when moving to Texas was the warmer winter. She hated snow. It was beautiful, but living in it was not fun.

She rested her head on the back of her seat and watched Paloma play. It'd be really easy to fall asleep. That wasn't good. "Let's sing some songs while we wait."

Paloma loved singing, so she pulled out every song she knew until she saw the big black truck driving their way.

She knew that being an independent, strong woman was a good thing, but sometimes it was really nice having someone you could count on. She wasn't sure why, but tears burned in her eyes. Hudson said that he would come, and now he was here.

As an adult, she had never had one single person she could truly depend on. This was his job, that was all, she reminded herself. She wasn't anyone special to him... and the sooner she got that through her thick skull, the better it would be for both of them.

Moments later, the black truck eased past her and stopped, its flashers on.

As Hudson walked around and inspected her car,

he looked like a man in control of his world. Then his gaze came up to hers and he smiled, coming to her door.

She opened it and got out. "Thank you so much for coming to get us."

He grinned and nodded. "Seems as if even a girl from Ohio needs help when it comes to Texas ice."

He walked around to get Paloma.

"It's ice no matter where you live, Sheriff Menchaca. I just didn't think we'd have ice on the road along the beach."

He lifted Paloma and her car seat out, wrapped in a blanket. "Reports are saying that every county in Texas is under a winter weather watch. First time in history. It's going to be a big mess. Since the ranch is closer, I'll drive you over there and we'll take care of your car later. Is that okay?"

"Works for me." She looked up and down the long stretch of road. "I don't think anyone is going to be out vandalizing or stealing cars right now."

He laughed. "You got that right. Careful." He helped her into the truck and handed her Paloma. "I'll get her car seat locked in. Anything else you need from the car?"

"Yes. The baskets. One is on the driver's side. The other two are in the back seat. Is it too much trouble to take them now? That was the whole reason I was going up to the ranch, anyway."

He lowered his chin and narrowed his eyes, the blue and gold taking her breath for a moment. Would she ever get used to his penetrating stare?

"Abigail. That is not the only reason. I would even say it's not the main reason. But it's a great excuse to go to the ranch and tell them who you are." He didn't say another word. Instead, he simply closed the door and went to the red car.

She stepped down from the truck and walked over to the passenger side of her car. Hudson already had the two larger baskets, and she grabbed the smaller one.

"Let's get going," he told her. "It's brutally cold out here."

With the baskets and Paloma settled in the back seat, they both got into the front. She hugged her coat closer to her. His truck was so warm.

"So have you thought of what you're going to say to them?"

"About the baskets?" She sat back and grinned. He was so serious that it was easy to tease him. With the predictability of the sun rising in the east, he shot her a glare and then turned back to keep his eyes on the road.

"No. I'm thinking along the lines of you telling them that you're Gabby, their baby sister."

She pulled in closer to herself. "You do know you take yourself way too seriously, right?"

"Have you been talking to my sisters?"

Laughter bubbled up, and Paloma joined in. "You've heard that before?"

"Unfortunately, yes, but stop trying to distract me."

"From what?" she asked innocently.

"You know what." He released a breath. "We were talking about you and the real reason you're going to the ranch."

Rubbing her hands over her arms, she looked out at the quickly changing landscape. "I've gone over it a million times. Should I tell them first, as soon as I get there? Then, after dinner, talk about the baskets and the opportunity of us working together? I'm really excited about that."

She took a deep breath. "But me being Gabby might overshadow the work stuff. So, I should start with that. After dinner, I can tell them who I am. Belle said the whole family was going to be there. The kids too? Who do I tell and when do I do it?"

With a heavy sigh, she leaned back against the seat.

"I wish I had an answer for you, but I don't," he admitted gruffly. "This is a decision you have to make for yourself."

They fell into silence, and he focused on the road. Hudson gripped the steering wheel, his jaw clenched. He drew in a deep breath, his chest expanding and his shoulders falling. The black gloves fitted snugly over his large hands.

It was clear he wanted to say something more. And she didn't want him to hold back for her sake. Because deep down she needed reassurance that she was doing the right thing.

"Hudson, I understand where you're coming from, but I really want to know what you recommend. Because I can see myself completely chickening out and not saying anything. Maybe you being here is a good thing. I know you won't let me leave without telling them the truth."

"Abigail, you have no idea what a big deal this will be to them. They've been worried about you for years. I know you have different memories of what happened." He blew out a breath. "And you asked for my advice so I'm going to give it to you. After dinner, take Belle or Xavier, whomever you're the most comfortable with, and ask to speak with them alone. Let them take you back to the family and introduce you. I think it would be less overwhelming."

"Xavier's my big brother. He taught me so much. He wasn't the one that put me in the car. Maybe he didn't know. I don't know what he knew. You're right… I was a nine-year-old, and the memories are blurred. What if they don't believe me?"

He nodded. "It's a possibility. That would be the only thing that would stop them from embracing you and welcoming you home. I'll let Xavier know it's okay for him to believe you. That'll be the hardest thing for them because, just like you, good things don't come easy for them. They've been taken advantage of and lied to by family. So, they might be a little skeptical that you've suddenly shown up. But that doesn't mean they don't love you. Either way, it seems as if your faith is solid. You know God has you."

"That's true. Thank you. So, you're saying that the worst-case scenario is they think I'm a con artist like Brady?" She laughed, and as she did, the weight lifted from her shoulders. "The irony of them thinking it's a con, right? But I can deal with that. If that's the only thing stopping us from moving forward, then that I understand. Hopefully they'll give me a chance to prove who I am."

"You also deserve answers. There are pieces of information you are missing. You were just a kid who got thrown out into the world alone. They wanted to protect you, but I think it went wrong. It wasn't because they didn't love you."

Did they love her? They didn't know her. Had she ever been truly loved just for herself? The dunes disappeared and she could see the gulf. More than an inch of snow covered the sand. "Can we stop?"

He slowed. "What is it? Something wrong?"

"No. But how often is it you see a beach covered in snow? It might not ever happen again. I want to take a picture. Is that okay?"

"For social media?" He made it sound like a disease.

"No. I stay far away from all that after everything that happened with my ex… It's for Paloma. She won't remember any of this."

When he came to a complete stop and put the truck in Park, she climbed down and made her way to the beach. A huge tree trunk was pushed up on the shore. The twisted roots were tangled with a blue rope that had to be four inches wide. Snow covered most of it. It looked like a piece of modern art, man versus nature.

Each shot had her full focus. She didn't hear Hudson come up behind her. "Let me take a picture of you."

With a small squeal, she spun around. "You scared me."

"Sorry." He didn't look sorry. Holding out his hand, he waited for her to hand over her phone.

Instead, she pointed it at him and snapped some photos. "The sheriff doing his job in an ice storm. Oh look! There are snowflakes on your hat." Lowering her phone, she scanned the winterized beach. "God is amazing. In the harshest conditions, He can show us beauty if we take the time to look around. I don't need a picture of me."

"Paloma will love seeing her mom way back when." He took her phone.

"It would be so cool to build a snowman castle. I need my gloves and scarf and earmuffs." She lifted her hands up to pose, and he took a picture of her standing in the snow in front of the ocean. He gave her the phone and started back to his truck. "Let's go. I think you might be stalling."

She scooped the snow off the top of the tree and balled it up. As he turned the corner of the truck, she struck him. Faster than she could blink, he turned to her. Muscles frozen, she stood, paralyzed. Why had she done that? Was he going to leave her here?

"Are you done?" he asked in a super calm voice. "Your daughter is waiting." He opened his door and paused for a minute. "I would return fire, but as you pointed out, you don't have the proper gear for a snowball fight."

With that, he got in the truck and waited for her. She shivered. She ran round to the passenger side and slammed the door behind her. "I'm sorry."

"You don't know how sorry you'll be for starting a war with me."

Was he grinning?

He then had the audacity to wink at her. "I might have grown up in Texas, but I've lived all over the world and I know how to win a snowball fight. I recommend you watch your back. Ambush is my favorite technique."

"You'll have to catch me first." She laughed.

Hudson wanted to chuckle out loud at her expression. How had he ever thought her pretentious and shallow? He hated to admit it, but his sisters might be right. He had become too serious.

Right now, all his focus was on his daughter. That was as it should be, but he needed balance also. Maybe he had been too narrow in his view of life. He could be friends with Abigail. That wouldn't risk Charlotte any more than making friends at school.

"How long have you and Xavier been friends?"

"About eight or nine years."

She glanced over at him. "He enlisted right after graduation? You said you served together?"

"Yep. He was such a kid. At seventeen, he was the youngest. But he was also the most determined. There was this huge chip on his shoulder, and he was the only one of us who was married."

"Selena. I remember them dating. They were insepa- rable. He said he was going to marry her. Are they going to be mad that I lied to them?" She turned away from him and looked out the window. His gaze flicked to the car seat in the back. Paloma was asleep.

"I don't know, but I do know he had two photos that went everywhere with him. One of Selena, and then the group picture you had. His family means everything to him, and he'd do anything to protect them. That would include you. They might be hurt that you've seen them in town and even talked to them but didn't say anything. Just like you need to give them a chance, they need to listen to you too."

He wanted to wrap her in his arms and tell her it was all going to work out, that this would have a happy ending, but he'd figured out long ago that no one could make that kind of promise.

As they rolled through the ranch gates, the back of the truck fishtailed. Abigail gripped the dashboard and turned to check on her daughter. Paloma was still sound asleep.

"Sorry." The truck straightened, and he eased forward.

"Have I mentioned I hate ice?" she said between clenched teeth. Scanning the snow-covered pastures, she tried to recall any memories, but she was coming up empty. She shook her head. "This doesn't look familiar."

"With all the snow, I don't recognize it either—and I was out here a couple of weeks ago."

"That's true. It's beautiful, but it's a lie, isn't it? It looks unblemished. The pure white blanket hides so much. I don't see any buildings."

"The main house is way back. There are several cabins. Damian and his wife have a place on the ranch. It's even farther back, closer to the coastline. I think they're out of town. They travel for her work."

"So, Damian won't be there. He's the only one I haven't seen in town." Her heart raced as they went deeper into the ranch. Snow made it surreal.

"He rarely comes to town. After he came back from the service, he pretty much became a recluse. There was an explosion during his last tour of duty, and he's a double amputee. The lower half of his left arm and leg had to be removed."

"What? That's horrible." She pulled the blanket over herself and huddled into it. "I've missed so much. Is he okay? They haven't had an easy time of it."

"No, none of them have, but they haven't let any of it hold them back. They're good people who have fought to come out on top. That's why I was a little protective of them before I knew what had brought you to our town."

She nodded. Her big eyes were sad as she scanned the landscape. "All my memories with them are good ones. Other than the last one with Belle and Elijah. That's why I was so hurt when they didn't come get me. I believed in them one hundred percent. But my aunt's constant tirades about them and them not coming to prove her wrong had me doubting my memories. I'm still not sure what's true and what's just part of my imagination." She sat straighter and pointed to the right. "Is that the house?"

"Yep." The sun was setting. Turning to drink it all in, he noted that the warm colors of the evening sky made everything shimmer in the ice and snow.

"Why am I so nervous?" Her gaze stayed on the horizon, but her hand reached for his.

He didn't think she even knew she was doing it. His fingers met hers, her smaller hand curling around them.

"You've got this." He wanted to promise her that it was going to be okay, but again he stopped short. He had no right to make any promises to her.

"Thank you for being here." She kept her face turned toward the house, but her fingers tightened around his.

It was as if she had a direct line to his heart. Why was this so difficult? He wasn't interested in a romantic relationship. So why did his heart and head act as if he had given them the go-ahead?

As soon as he knew she was safe and that the De La Rosa family had taken her in, he would be out of here. There was a county that needed him.

He didn't have time to be distracted by one lost woman. She would find her way without him. She had to.

Chapter Thirteen

"I remember the porch." Her rapid pulse was visible in her neck.

"This is it. My childhood home." She practically had her face pressed against the glass.

"The drive goes around to the back of the house and to the main barn. I'd follow my dad and Xavier and beg to get a horse. Sometimes they would take me out with them. Most of the time I was sent back to the house to help my mother." She glanced over at him with a half attempt at a smile. "I'd get so mad and kick dirt clods all the way to the kitchen door. Sometimes I'd hide in the garden just to prove they couldn't tell me what to do." She went on, eyes wide. "The garden was my favorite place. It was huge with vined-in areas that made a perfect hiding spot. I hid there a lot whenever I was mad or scared."

Sadness pulled at his heart. The idea of a small Abigail hiding hurt him. "Do you remember why you were scared?"

She was quiet for a moment, her eyes shadowed as she tried to recall the memories. Shaking her head, she looked back to the house. He eased the truck as close to the front porch as he could manage. The less she had to walk on the icy ground, the better.

She gasped and covered her mouth with her hand. "Mamma. I can see her standing on the top step."

Now he was concerned. "You see her right now?"

She laughed. "No. My memory of her standing there is so clear, it's like I could reach out to her."

He sighed in relief. At least she had more of a grin back.

"Don't worry, Sheriff. I haven't slipped into a hallucination." She pointed to the post at the top of the steps. "In the mornings she would stay there until we were out of sight. Xavier drove us to the bus stop at the end of our ranch road. In the afternoons, she would be waiting in the same spot. When I first went to school, I thought Mamma stood there all day, her life on hold until we came home. I wanted to stay with her so she wouldn't be alone, but of course they didn't let me."

"Did you tell them why you wanted to stay?"

She pursed her lips and tilted her head. "That I don't remember." She snorted. "It also didn't occur to me that a mom raising five kids needed downtime."

"Your world revolved around your mom, and you kids were her world. She probably did miss you. Xavier and the others have wonderful memories of your mother. She sounded like a very loving person."

"Thank you. Sometimes when I was in the fourth grade, she wasn't there on the porch, and I was happy that she'd found other things to do. There was always a snack waiting for us in the kitchen, and dinner would be started. I would help Belle finish it. Mamma was so tired. She would be in bed when we got home. I was so clueless. I was happy that she had so much new stuff to do that she was tired. I thought that her new stuff must really be fun if it made her go to bed so early. I would curl up with her and do my homework, and she would read to me. Every night." She took a deep breath. A tear fell on her hand, and she seemed surprised by its presence.

"Oh sorry. I didn't mean to do that." Sniffing, she wiped her face. "I wasn't expecting to be hit with emotions like this." She shook her head and tapped her cheeks with her fingers. "Do I look okay?"

"You've been stuck in an ice storm with your baby." He cupped the side of her head with his hand. His thumb wiped the trail of tears off. She was beautiful, but he didn't think she needed to hear that from him. Plus, he absolutely didn't need to be saying it, let alone thinking it.

"They're the most unjudgmental people you'll ever meet. They aren't going to think anything about this. Besides, you were so young when they sent you away. I don't think you ever got the chance to properly grieve. Do you want to tell them right away and get it over with?"

"No." She looked as if she wanted to throw up. "I need to stick to the plan."

"Do you want me to carry Paloma or the gift baskets? Which do you want to take?"

"I'll take the baskets and focus on the job. Otherwise, I might completely forget the reason I'm here. If you'd watch Paloma, that would help me stay focused. I think if I have her, it will be more personal and I'll lose it."

"It's okay to lose it sometimes." He sat back and gave her space. "Like when you're reunited with a family you haven't seen since the day you buried your mother. You were a child, Abigail. There's a lot of emotions to process."

"Now you sound like a psychologist. Is that part of your sheriff training?"

"Nope. It's years of counseling my father forced on me because I was an angry teenager and he didn't have a clue what to do with me."

Her lips quirked. "That was smart of him."

"Yeah. It was also a way to handle me without actually talking to me himself. After the murder of my mom, our relationship was rocky at best."

"Have you talked now?"

"Not really. My father is a fixer. Not much into talking about it. Just fix it and move on. He's really good at moving on." An uncomfortable tightness squeezed his chest whenever he talked about his father. He loved the man so much, but he also hated him.

Despite the therapy and his sisters, he couldn't shake the belief that his mother's death was his fault. His father had to blame him, even if he never said it. If his mother was still alive, they would never have gone down this path. "When did this become about me?"

"When you started giving me advice on talking to family."

"Smart mouth."

"My mamma would say it's better than being a dumb one."

Laughter erupted from him at the unexpected reply. Paloma's eyes opened. "Ma. Ma. Ma."

"It's okay, sweetheart. We're here."

The front door opened, and Belle De La Rosa stepped onto the porch.

"We're home." Tears hovered on the edge of Abigail's words.

"Think about the baskets for now, or you'll never get through this."

She nodded and stiffened her spine before opening her door. He got out and went to get Paloma.

Belle waved as she came down the steps. She wore thick work gloves on her hands. "I'm glad to see y'all. This weather has turned into a monster. Careful of the ice. The beautiful snow is covering it up." The whirling snow was so thick it became harder to see. "Here, let me help."

She took two of the baskets from Abigail. "This is some customer service. Let's get that baby inside where it's warm. And both of you. You are staying here where it is safe and warm."

"Thank you so much." Abigail followed Belle, and Hudson stayed right behind her. "We'd still be stuck out there if Hudson hadn't rescued us."

Paloma was cocooned in several layers of clothes and a blanket. It was hard to tell there was a baby buried beneath all that. She definitely had her daughter prepared for the cold.

He tried to tell her that, but a gust of cold air hit and made it impossible to talk. He'd need something to cover his face if this kept up. It wasn't even nightfall yet and it would only get colder.

The snow crunched under their boots as they made their way into the house. The warm air felt good. They hadn't been out long, but the temperature had to have dropped since he checked last. "We're going to be in for a long winter night."

Belle nodded. "My husband, Quinn, and cousin

Xavier, are making sure the stock has water and shelter. My brother Elijah and his wife Jazmine are adding a heater in the pump house and wrapping the exposed pipes. We also have all the tubs full of water in case the pipes freeze. They're predicting that it's going to get worse by tomorrow afternoon and that we might not get above freezing for three or four days. Not sure our system can handle that."

"We've never seen anything like this. It's going to be a mess across the state," Hudson murmured.

"Yes. We're ready to hunker down. All the kids are snuggled in the family room under a big tent." She turned toward Abigail. "Be warned. We tend to be loud and all over the place, but I like to call it controlled chaos."

Hudson placed his hand on her back and guided her through the living room. It was warm and comforting and very lived-in. The love in the house wrapped around her.

But there was nothing from her memories; she didn't recognize it as the house she grew up in. They followed Belle into a huge country kitchen. Emotions threatened to overwhelm her. Hudson's hand slid to hers, and he gave it a gentle squeeze.

Abigail took a deep breath and grounded herself. They were here to talk about ideas for the Dulce Panadería and the short-term rental cabins. This was a business meeting so they could work together to increase traffic and outside sales.

She would put on her fake happy for a few more hours. Her ability to pretend everything was great had been honed after years of survival and trying to fit in.

Once she told them the truth, she was never going to fake her way through life again.

After tonight, she was going to address any problem head-on, then move past it. No more wasting time feigning that everything was fine when it wasn't.

Yes. That was her new mantra: address the problem, then move on. She could do this. Everything inside her shook, but that was okay. This was a big event in her life. It was normal to feel uncertain.

God, I know You have this and I trust You will be holding on to me no matter what happens tonight.

Belle stopped at a large rustic farm table. That hadn't been here when she lived here. There were twelve chairs spaced comfortably around it, and the smell of fresh bread and other appetizing aromas filled the room. She saw an older woman at the stove. Belle introduced her as her mother-in-law.

The kitchen was modernized and new. She didn't remember it being this big or having an island.

"This is a great kitchen. It looks a lot newer than the rest of the house."

"It's a complete redo. We knocked out some walls and redesigned it. This is the heart of our home. I spent hours learning to cook in the old ranch kitchen with my mother. She talked about remodeling all the time. I'd like to think she'd approve."

Hudson was next to her. "Belle is a great cook. Everyone says yes if they get invited to have dinner at the ranch, even if it means rearranging everything else. Thank you for including me."

She laughed. "You're always invited, Sheriff. I'm not sure I'm up to the Espinoza standard and I know they've been feeding you. But I don't think we had much choice tonight. Mother Nature is in charge. But I'm glad you're both here. These baskets are amazing. I can't wait to show them to everyone."

"Is that fresh bread I smell?"

"Yes. This is most certainly bread-baking weather. I've made cinnamon rolls for the morning."

The back door opened, and Abigail heard stamping feet and talking. She had met everyone in town at one point other than Elijah and Damian. She had seen them at church.

As they came in from the back porch, the room was filled with energy and laughter. "I told you he was going to do that," Jazmine was saying as they walked in.

Selena, Xavier's wife, came in from the front room, then went straight to Abigail and hugged her. "We're so glad you made it. We were worried. I've been listening to the reports." She turned to Hudson and took Paloma's hand. The baby curled her fingers around Selena's. "We've closed all the roads and asked people to stay wherever they're at. It's going to be a rough night. The bad weather came in so fast. Abigail, I know you're from Ohio, but ice always makes me nervous."

Xavier came in behind his wife and wrapped his arms around her. "When it comes to everyone's safety, she's always nervous."

She sighed and leaned into her husband. "This is true, but it's getting bad out there."

"It is." Abigail smiled at Hudson. He was holding Paloma as if it was the most natural thing in the world. "I'm thankful that the sheriff was able to get to us."

"We would have gotten you, no worries." Elijah was studying her, his head tilted. "Do I know you from somewhere? You're new to Port Del Mar?"

Hudson moved closer to her and put his free hand on her arm. "She's working for the Espinoza family and has been going to church. I want to thank you for inviting us to stay. I know Abigail doesn't want to take Paloma out in this storm."

"Oh, don't even think about it." Belle waved him off. "We have plenty of room. It might be a little crowded, but that's better for staying warm, right? Come on, let's sit. We have a little time before the kids come in asking for dinner, so tell us about the baskets and how you see us working together."

Selena sat at the table. "If Belle had her way, everyone would live at the ranch all the time. There're never enough people on the ranch for her."

Elijah snorted as he started looking through one of the baskets. "That's the truth. I wouldn't put it past her to call up a storm just so we all have to stay longer."

Everyone laughed. Belle waved a wooden spoon in the air. "Yes. My powers are great, and I have control over the weather. If my family is wise, they will do as I say."

Elijah pulled off a piece of fresh bread and popped it in his mouth. "We already do what you say."

"Not always, but my little brother is learning well."

Jazmine wrapped her arms around Abigail and pulled her to the table. "Ignore them. Do you have siblings?"

She froze. If she said no, that would be an outright lie and she couldn't do that. "I do."

"I've got twin sisters that put any sibling rivalry to shame," Hudson said as he sat and balanced Paloma on his knee. "So why the three baskets? Wouldn't one work?"

She loved him. Wait, no. She didn't *love* him. She strongly appreciated his attempt to steer the conversation back to the business.

"Selena, Belle and I have been talking about doing something unique, and when Belle said you had been thinking the same thing but even bigger, we got very excited." Jazmine turned to her husband, Elijah. "It would even benefit our other businesses."

"That's right." Selena smiled. "We could pull in all the local shops and farms. The welcome baskets would be put together based on visitors' interests. I think one of the best parts of Abigail's idea is that people can preorder items to add to them."

Elijah pulled a paper fish from the basket closest to him. "Someone could book a deep-sea fishing trip ahead and the details would be waiting for them on their arrival?"

Selena gave Abigail an apologetic look. "Sorry. I just love the possibilities of your idea."

"I'm so happy you're excited. But to answer your question, Elijah…yes, it could be a deep-sea fishing expedition. Or, alternatively, it could be a birthday party on the pirate ship. In that case, the basket would be designed for the birthday kid. Or if it's a girls' weekend, there could be spa supplies or horse riding. I thought we could have a birthday package, a romantic weekend package, and a guys' or girls' getaway, along with the standard family vacation. I'm open to other ideas too." She paused to take a breath. "The packages could have different budget levels and, since the customers are booking ahead, there could be discounts. Everything they want would all be waiting for them in their custom basket with detailed instructions, maps and numbers. All they have to do is enjoy."

Selena stood and went to a basket. "It would really benefit the whole community and bring in more revenue."

"How would this all work? Have you talked to other businesses?" Xavier asked her.

Letting her excitement for this project take over, Abigail explained the details and how they would work together to do it. She would be the point person, organizing and delivering the final basket to each cabin. Elaborating further, she told them she'd created a forecast, a profit analysis and a list of potential problems.

Time slipped past as she answered questions and they explored all the opportunities. The De La Rosa family was going through the baskets now, making suggestions and picking out the things they really liked.

For the first time since they'd started, she looked over at the corner of the table. Hudson had made a comment or two, but he had mostly been keeping Paloma amused. She couldn't help mentally comparing him to her ex-husband, who had always needed to be the center of attention. It had been her job to make sure he looked good.

It had been clear from the first day that Hudson was nothing like her ex, but it went deeper than just being a good man of honor. When he took care of people, it wasn't for his own benefit. He truly respected and valued those around him.

He caught her staring at him and immediately grinned, then gave her a thumbs-up. Her heart kicked against her chest. *No*, she told herself, *he's just being friendly. He helps people for a living. It doesn't mean anything.*

Three of the older kids came in to save her from her spiraling thoughts. They were Quinn and Belle's oldest, asking about dinner.

Elijah and Xavier gathered dishes and Belle removed a few items from the oven and put them in a box. Everything was set for the kids to have a picnic in their fort. Jazmine and Elijah took the dinner to the other room as Belle and Quinn set the table for the adults.

Everyone worked so well together, like this big family dinner was a normal routine. They'd embraced her marketing plan, but that didn't mean they wanted Gabby De La Rosa back at their table.

She sat on the other side of Paloma. "Thank you for watching her."

"Not a problem. Charlotte is at a fun age, but I do miss her being a baby. It goes by so fast." He studied the activity in the kitchen for a minute. "Who are you going to talk to first?"

"My first thought was Xavier. He's my oldest brother, and as I mentioned, he wasn't there when I was dragged into the car. But then there's Belle. She's like a sister to me. We shared a room. She's been the friendliest."

"What are you two whispering about?" Jazmine had come back into the room and was pulling out the chair next to Abigail.

"Jazmine. Leave them alone." Belle set a platter of fajita steak on the table.

As the family joined hands to pray, Abigail had to stop herself from crying. This was a dream she had held in her heart for so long, and it had become reality thanks to Hudson.

Without him pushing her, she would have kept talking herself out of doing this. She might have still backed out if it weren't for the ice storm sending him to her rescue. God knew what she needed before she did.

Talk of the weather and what needed to be done for the ranch, a few jokes, and a plethora of shared memories kept the conversation going until everyone was finished eating.

Elijah stood and started gathering empty plates. "The sooner the table is cleared, the sooner we get dessert."

"That's true, but you also hate a mess." His wife laughed and helped him clear the table.

Hudson nodded at Abigail. She took a deep breath and went to Belle. "Is there somewhere we can talk? I have something personal to tell you."

Quinn was watching them, and Abigail almost told her to forget it. But Belle reached for her as she was backing up. "Sure. Would the front room be private enough? We could go to the screened-in porch, but it's a bit cold."

"The living room is fine." She glanced at Hudson as she followed her cousin. He was standing, bouncing Paloma. He gave her a wink, then turned to Xavier.

"Is everything all right?" Belle asked once they were alone, her voice coated with concern. "How can I help?"

"I haven't been truthful about who I am."

Leaning her head to the side, Belle narrowed her eyes. "You're not Abigail Dixon?"

"I am. But I've lived in Port Del Mar before. I'm Gabby De—"

Her words were cut off by a tackling hug. Her ears rang from the scream. Everyone rushed in from the kitchen. Everyone but Hudson.

"What happened?" someone out of her line of vision asked.

"Gabby's home!" Belle still had her in a hug. Abigail couldn't move her arms.

"I knew she looked familiar. I told you I knew her from somewhere." Elijah was next to her. "Belle, you have to let her go."

"No, I don't. I'm never letting her go." But she did. Belle was crying.

Elijah was the next to hug her, then Selena and Jazmine. "Where have you been? Why have you been hiding from us? What happened after you left, where'd you go? We've been so worried about you."

The questions came from all sides as they passed her around. Belle took her hand and led her to the couch. The kids came in wanting to know what had happened and were told that their missing aunt had come home. The children all hugged Abigail too. They had been told about her and were excited. But now they wanted to take their new cousin with them to the fort. Quinn's mother took Paloma and went with them.

Hudson stood close by, but he still hadn't said anything. Xavier, who hadn't embraced her yet, turned to his friend. "You knew?"

He gave him a quick nod. "For about a week now."

With a flick of his shoulder, Xavier glared at him. "You didn't think I would want to know that my baby sister was safe and here in town?"

Abigail stood. "As soon as he found out, he told me that if I didn't tell you, he would. Don't be mad at him."

Xavier turned to her. Something between anger and hurt was etched into his face. "Why did you have to be pressured to tell us you were here?"

She looked around at her brother and cousins, their wives. They waited for her response. "Because I don't understand the reason you sent me away. Mamma was gone and they—" she waved her hand to Elijah and Belle "—made me leave with a woman I didn't know. I clung to Elijah and begged Belle. I yelled for you. Where were you? Why did y'all send me away?" Now she was crying, almost sobbing. Hudson stood behind her and put an arm around her, holding her close to him.

"I thought you loved me. Tía said you were all evil and that it was a good thing she saved me. I told her—" a sob interrupted her words "—I told her you were coming for me. I had my backpack hidden under my bed. You never came. Why? I didn't even know Daddy had died. Xavier, you said you'd..." She couldn't say another word.

Hudson's arm tightened around her. Xavier reached for her, his hand cupping her face. "Oh, baby girl. I said I'd always love you and protect you, and I did. Our father was a mean drunk. Mamma was afraid he would lose all control when she died, and he did. We did everything we could to keep you out of his way, but we were afraid we couldn't always be there. We asked Tía to take you for a few months until we could figure something out. It took longer than we thought." Tears rolled down his handsome face.

Belle took her hand, with Elijah right next to her. "Gabby, Xavier had the hardest time staying away that day. But he was afraid if he went that you'd ask him to let you stay and he would give in. We all decided with Mamma that you had to be safe and that the only place to send you was with Tía. We called. She would tell us to stop. We didn't. But then the number was disconnected. Nine months later, we couldn't take it anymore, so Xavier, Damian and I drove to get you and bring you home. You weren't there. We lost all track of you. We were still all in school, so there wasn't anything we could do."

Belle hugged her again, pulling her away from Hudson. "I'm so sorry you felt abandoned. I prayed that you were loved and happy. Frank just got worse. On the worse days, I'd picture you happy and loved and grateful we found you another home. He drove all the boys away. It was miserable. I was glad you didn't have to go through that." Belle released her and had to wipe the tears off her face.

Xavier took her hand and, for a long moment, everyone was quiet as he stared at her. "I should have seen it. You look like Mamma. We all look like the De La Rosa side." His eyes glistened with moisture. He glanced to the door where the kids were. "Paloma has the De La Rosa eyes."

"She does."

"I've prayed for your happiness and safety. I figured if you didn't want to find us, then you were happy. You were always in my heart, baby sister. I'm so, so sorry I didn't protect you like I promised, but I never, ever stopped loving you." He pulled her into his arms, engulfing her. Cocooned by Xavier, she clung to him.

She was home. They had not stopped loving her. Hudson had been right all along. God had brought her home.

"Damian!" Belle cried. "We have to call him. Use the video so he can see her."

It was after two in the morning before sleepiness interrupted their conversation. The kids had been put to bed hours ago, and at one point Abigail realized that Hudson had slipped out of the room. She sat at the kitchen table with Xavier, Belle and Elijah. They had just hung up from chatting with Damian.

Belle leaned in and rested her head on her shoulder. "You are not alone any longer, and you have choices. Think about what you want to do, and we'll support you."

Abigail nodded. She was overwhelmed by all the choices. No matter what she did, her daughter now had family. *She* had family.

Chapter Fourteen

It had been a long, hard week since Hudson had rescued Abigail from the embankment. He hadn't seen her for the last four days. But the sun was out, and the ice and snow were finally gone.

Walking around the side of the De La Rosa house, he found her where Belle had said she would be. Her back was to him. She was wrapped in a blanket and sitting on a bench swing that hung from the branch of a giant live oak.

The weather had been worse than anyone had predicted. The snow and ice had been unprecedented across Texas. Several times he'd been thankful that he had brought her out here to the Diamondback Ranch.

The utilities in town had been down and the water lines had frozen. The ranch had been more prepared for off-grid survival than her apartment.

He watched her for a while. She had no clue what an amazing woman she was. Most people would have crumpled under her burdens. The morning sun was highlighting the red in her dark hair. It fell in loose waves around her neck, natural and beautiful.

He took a step closer and she turned. A smile glowed in her eyes. "Well, hello, cowboy. Long time no see. Everyone safe in the county?"

"Back to normal for now. Hard to believe that this was all covered in snow and ice less than twenty-four hours ago."

She scooted over, giving him room to sit. "It's surreal. I was afraid that when the snow melted, I would find myself alone again." She smiled and took a sip of her coffee. "I don't think I have to worry about that anymore. Belle's trying to get me to move out here."

He tried not to frown, but his first thought was that she would be farther from home. Farther from him. Biting back a growl, he turned his gaze to the ranch. A few horses were standing at the fence, enjoying the sun.

When had he started associating her with home? He sighed. Falling in love with her was a mistake; he wouldn't make it worse by telling her. He knew better than anyone that life wasn't easy and that you rarely got what you wanted. "So, are you moving out here?"

"Oh no." She laughed. "I love them, but I've gotten really used to quiet. There is nothing quiet about this house."

A truck came up the drive. When she turned to see who it was, it put her closer to him. He fought the urge to pull her against him.

"It's Xavier." She didn't seem to notice that she snuggled into him. He waved and they waved back. They watched in silence as he made his way to the house.

"You know, I've never actually been on my own. I thought it would be horrible. But I've enjoyed settling in at my apartment with Paloma. I love that we have our own space. It means even more now that I know my family loves me."

With a nod, he draped an arm over her shoulder. She fit against him so naturally.

"Thank you, Hudson. I have so many options now."

"I didn't do anything." Her gratitude made his skin too tight.

"Do you know that the De La Rosas had set aside an account for me? I own a part of the ranch, which I haven't actually wrapped my brain around yet. But there's money for me to go back to finish college. It's all a bit overwhelming."

Everything inside him stilled. She was going even farther away?

"Where would you go?" The question burned his throat.

"I don't know, that's the beauty of it. I could go any-where. I could finish at Ohio State. I had two semesters there before I moved in with Brady."

He kept his focus on the horizon. Yeah, her moving to the ranch would have been a better option than Ohio. But for the first time, she was able to make choices for herself. This was important. So, he made sure to nod and keep his voice casual. "You're a Buckeye?"

"I guess. But I'm not really feeling it." She took a sip of coffee. "It's the obvious choice, but it feels like going backward. I don't have any good memories there, other than Paloma."

His next breath came a little easier, the tightness in his chest loosening. "Options are always good. You have an amazing talent. I saw it in action earlier this week. You've basically started your own business with nothing. Is there a reason that you want to finish school?"

"I've never done anything on my own except leave for college. I had applied for a ton of scholarships and I had to work really hard, but then I let Brady save me. Of course, looking back, I know now he wasn't doing me any favors."

Hudson wrapped his arm tighter around her and pulled her in. He kissed the top of her head. What he really wanted to do was protect her from the world. But everyone had lessons to learn, choices to make, a life to figure out. This was her time for that.

Shifting in her seat, she turned from the horizon to him. For a long moment, she just studied him.

His heart hit against his ribs. The stupid thing didn't understand that he couldn't have her. "What is it?"

"You know, when Brady came into my life, I thought he was saving me. But he wasn't—it was just another trap and I owed him. In exchange for his—" she paused and made air quotes "—'love,' I had to perform. I gave up everything I really was to make sure that I made him look good. That's all I was. But you…" She blinked a couple of times, and he looked away. She obviously didn't want to cry in front of him.

He gave her arm a quick squeeze and pressed his lips to her temple.

With a deep breath, she started again. "Thank you for rescuing me time and time again but not expecting anything in return."

She was breaking his heart. "We all need some help every once in a while. You helped me too."

She slapped him on the arm. "Liar. How have I ever helped you?"

"Several ways." He couldn't tell her that she'd brought his heart back to life when he hadn't even known it was hibernating. "You called me out and reminded me to talk to my dad. There was so much unsaid between us because it was difficult. I'm not using that as an excuse anymore. I called him and made some big steps in getting him back into my life.

"You also showed me that it's okay to make new friends. My list doesn't have to be short if I trust God. Trusting others, even God, to take care of the people I love is a hard thing to do. Thank you."

She bit her lip and nodded, then turned back to the horizon. "It's not easy to trust others, to open up and let them know you need help. It's so much easier to go about pretending everything's okay. It's hard to be honest, even with yourself, about not being okay."

Twisting to face him, she tilted her chin up. Her gaze holding his, she pulled him closer to her. He reached up and cupped his hand around her neck.

He didn't want to think about the past or future. This moment was all he wanted. He lowered his head slowly, and their lips touched, dancing with the softness of snowflakes on the breeze. He traced kisses to the corner of her mouth and back to the center. She was sweeter than even his imagination. Until this moment, he hadn't realized how much he had missed this kind of connection, but it wasn't just the kissing. It was her.

Abigail made him want to risk his heart all over again. To fall into the bottomless gulf. No, he couldn't do this to either one of them. They were going in different directions.

He forced himself to pull away, but he wasn't strong

enough to completely break contact. So he rested his forehead against hers. This had to stop, but his heart was singing. She could be his if he asked, but that wasn't fair to her. Not now, when the whole world was at her door.

"Hudson?" Her soft voice was unsure. He had done that.

"I'm sorry. That was a mistake." He stood, keeping his back to her. If he stayed that close, he'd start kissing her again, so he stared at the vast horizon. "I had your car driven to your apartment. The water and electricity are back on too. Are you ready to go home?"

"Yes."

Her touch on the sleeve of his Carhartt coat brought him back to her. "Hudson? What just happened?"

"It's been a long week, and I'm running on fumes. Let's go get Paloma and you can tell everyone goodbye. Unless you want to stay longer."

"I'm ready to go home."

Abigail's world was forever changed. Her family had been looking for her and loved her. Then Hudson had kissed her. Not just any kiss either. At least not for her. Maybe to him it was just an accident, but that kiss had shaken her foundation.

The trip back to town was thick with silence. How did they get back to their friendly conversations? She had shared more with him than she had with anyone else, but he had made it clear he wasn't interested in a relationship of any kind. And then he had talked about his list getting longer and kissed her.

She was so confused. With another glance at his profile, she tried to figure out what to say or do. Did this mean there was a chance that he was open to more from her, or was she looking for hints that weren't there?

His phone chimed. He reached over and hit Accept on his dashboard. "Hey, Madison."

Sweet laughter came over the speakers. "I tricked you, Daddy. It's me, Charlotte! I have a surprise for you. When are you coming home?"

"I'm going to drop Abigail and Paloma off at their place, then I'm coming home. Everything okay?"

"Yes. Please bring them. I want them to see my surprise too."

He glanced at Abigail with his brows raised in question. She nodded. "Sure." The word stuck in her dry throat.

"Yay!" Charlotte asked them questions and chatted for a while.

"Hey, little bear. I'm going to hang up now. I love you and we'll be there soon."

Silence fell over them again. She checked on her daughter. Breathing was becoming hard. She had to say something or explode. He might be the strong and silent type, but she needed words.

"Why did you kiss me?" Heat burned her neck. *Great.* In the next few minutes, her face would be red. This was why she never confronted anyone. It was so embarrassing.

The only indication that he had heard her was the flexing of his jaw and the white knuckles gripping the steering wheel. She waited. There was no backing out now.

"Hudson… I'm confused."

He sighed, his big shoulders falling. "Me too. I was tired, you were … I don't know. It shouldn't have happened, and I'm sorry. You have so much to decide right now. The last thing you need is me throwing more on your plate."

"Maybe I can make room. It's a big plate."

He grinned for the first time since he broke the kiss. "My issues are too big for anyone's plate. You have new fresh choices to make."

Her heart thumped. Was he saying he wanted to be one of her options? "Hudson."

"No. I have to focus on my daughter. She's only six, and she deserves my full attention. We're friends. That's all we can be."

"Did you just friend-zone me? A man who claimed he didn't want any more friends?"

He rolled his eyes as he drove slowly past the row of brightly colored beach homes. He pulled his truck under his pretty turquoise one with the white trim. She might love his house as much as she loved him.

She smiled, admitting to herself that she loved *him*. For the first time, she thought that maybe there was a chance.

He frowned, looking over her shoulder. Turning, she followed his gaze. "What is it?"

"That's my dad's Land Rover." He didn't seem happy that his father had made a surprise visit.

"I thought you said you called him."

"I did. But I didn't invite him over." He shook his head.

"But this is good, right?" she asked.

Getting out of the truck, he handed her the diaper bag and went to get Paloma. "I hope my sisters are all right."

She hadn't thought of that. "I just assumed he was the surprise Charlotte was excited about."

He nodded. "You're right. But why is he here?" Unlocking the tall gate, he held it open for her.

"Because his son called to have a real conversation after too many years?"

He grumbled under his breath as he followed her up the steps. "It's just weird. He's never been here before. The least he could have done was let me know he was coming."

Hudson opened the door for her. Inside, his family was waiting. "Surprise!"

Abigail blinked. There were balloons, a sign and a cake. "It's your birthday?"

"No." Shaking his head, he lifted his daughter with his free arm as she threw herself at him.

"Happy Birthday, Daddy!" She hugged his neck and kissed his cheek.

Abigail lifted a brow and took her daughter from him. "It's not?"

Madison and Liberty rushed over to them. They hugged her, then their brother. "His birthday is Monday. But he probably forgot. He does that when he's busy. He forgets everything."

He sighed. "It's true."

They led him to the table, where his dad stood, not looking very sure of his welcome. "Son. Happy birthday. Your mom always thought this day should be a big family celebration. You joining us and all."

"I remember."

Abigail's heart hurt. His birthday had become another reminder of what they had lost.

"PaPa brought the cake. He said German chocolate was your favorite. Margarita made it for you. She said it won't be as good as your mom's, but she did her best. Right, PaPa?"

"Yes, ma'am. I suspect it will be super close. Is it okay? Me, being here—"

Hudson cut his dad off with a real hug this time, and the two men clung to each other. The sisters, close to tears, made themselves busy getting plates and drinks.

Stepping back, Hudson wiped his face. "Thank you, Dad. This is great."

"PaPa, this is Paloma and Ms. Abigail. They're our new friends. Paloma and I want to be sisters." His family laughed. Abigail and Hudson did not.

Cake was served and funny stories of Hudson were shared. Then Charlotte wanted to show Paloma the new doll and clothes her aunts had given her.

Liberty had whispered to Abigail that Hudson and their father had ignored their birthdays since their mother died, confirming what Abigail had suspected. Remembering his birthday was painful for both father and son.

Abigail was reluctant to leave Hudson's side. Was it her imagination, or had he leaned on her several times during the little celebration? She wanted to help him like he'd helped her. But he had just told her that he had to focus on his daughter, and she understood that. He had offered her friendship, and she'd have to be happy with that.

He had his own wounds, just like she did. With Paloma in her arms, she followed the girls to Charlotte's room. She paused once to glance back at him. She thought she caught him looking at her, but then he turned to his father so fast she thought maybe she had imagined it.

Then again, even the people who seemed the most put together could have scars hidden under all their perfect layers.

Chapter Fifteen

Abigail had just caught him staring at her. No wonder she was confused. He was sending her so many mixed messages and he had to stop. Set his mind right. Abigail was amazing, but if he started a relationship with her and then she left, his daughter would pay the highest price.

"That's quite a girl you got there." His dad pulled him back to the present.

"Not my girl."

"Well, that's a shame. Your sisters speak highly of her, and your daughter won't talk about anyone else but Ms. Abigail and Paloma."

"But we know how that will end, don't we?"

His father furrowed his brow. "I'm not sure I understand. You think she's a user and leaver like Zoe?"

"No. She's nothing like her." Hudson may have thought that the first week or so, but after spending time with her, he knew she had nothing in common with Zoe.

"Then how do you think it has to end?" His dad put down his fork and turned to him. "It's been a long time since we truly talked. Thank you for calling me the other day. I know it will take more than one conversation, but I want us to move forward. Being open and honest can be...difficult. But it was long overdue." He sighed and lowered his head for a bit. Then, with a deep breath, he locked his gaze with Hudson's.

"I thought about everything you told me. It was nothing I didn't already know. The police report contained everything you said. But I had no idea you blamed yourself for your mom's death. Or believed I held you responsible." His voice cracked. "I was dealing with a lot of grief, but I never, ever blamed you, son. It was just too painful to talk about and you were so angry. Emotions are hard. It was easier to send you to therapy."

"Thank you for that. I know at the time I yelled and fought, but overall, I can't imagine the choices I would have made if I hadn't had my therapist to guide me through the worst of it."

"But I still needed to talk to you. I was a coward." His father's lips were tight as he stared off into space. "Don't believe for a minute that your mother would've been okay coming home without you. I lost my partner, my best friend, the love of my life, but to lose a child? I thank God and your mother every night for making sure you came back to me."

Hudson's chest was tight. He had never thought of it that way. His father gripped his shoulder. "You have a daughter, now. What would you do to protect Charlotte?"

He'd lay down his life for his baby girl. Blinking back tears, he thought of his mother.

"Don't let her love for you get lost in bitterness and

guilt. Be happy and love every minute of this life she gave you, twice. That's what your mother wanted for you."

His father gripped the back of his head and pressed their foreheads together before pulling him into a bear hug. "Son, I love you so much."

Hudson didn't know how long they cried. But all the tears that had been pushed down and locked away were freed. They fell until his dad's shirt was saturated. Pulling back, he went to the sink and splashed his face. Going back to his dad, he offered him a clean towel.

His phone pinged. Pulling it out, he read the message and smiled. "The girls decided to go for a long walk on the beach."

His father nodded. "You know this was your mom's favorite time of year to visit the coast. She loved the off-season."

"I remember." Hudson nodded to his living room wall, where he had several family pictures. "Those are some of my favorite memories."

"Is your mom's death the reason you avoid real relationships?"

"Dad, I've been married. You were there. I know you never liked her, but that was a relationship. While it lasted, anyway."

"I never believed you were in love with Zoe," his father said. "She was a liar and con artist. You were tricked into that marriage, but we have Charlotte. So, like the Good Book says, God works it all for His good. But I'm talking about you falling in love, really caring for a woman. Putting yourself out there."

Hudson shrugged. After this emotional black hole they had just climbed out of, he owed it to his dad to be honest—but really, how much could they take in one night?

He sighed. On the other hand, maybe tonight was the night to get it all off their chests so they could finally move forward.

"Zoe messed me up some, but it's more than that, or Mom's death. It's a promise I made to Charlotte when she was born." He paused. Would this destroy the fragile communications they just started?

"Son. I want to help make this right. Talk to me."

Hudson leaned back. "After Mom died, you started dating right away."

Frowning, his dad shook his head. "It was close to a year. Maybe a little less. But I wasn't really dating. Clair was the first...she was a friend of ours and I could talk to her about your mother without feeling guilty."

"It looked like dating to me. You went out to dinner and movies. You even went dancing. You used to dance with Mom in the kitchen, and then you replaced her without a blink."

"Oh, Hudson." His brow wrinkled in a deep frown. "I'm sorry. I never thought about it like that. I missed your mom so much. I was drowning in darkness, but I had you kids, so I couldn't let it pull me down. I needed someone to talk to like I used to with your mom. I missed having a companion. I had you three kids and you were so angry that I had to figure out a way to stay present for y'all."

He shook his head. "Son, I've never stopped loving her. I'll never stop grieving her loss. But, um...dating, for lack of a better term, helped me. Do you remember me and your mom had date nights every week? Clair knew this. She'd come over and drag me out of the house. She wanted to be there for your sisters too. She was a good friend.

"I got better and even went out on some real dates. I think Abby lasted the longest, but the woman sitting across from me was never my wife and we'd always end up as friends. We can always use more friends, right? I also thought the twins could use some trusted female advice. They were coming to an age that feminine issues would need to be addressed. I grew up with brothers. Maybe that was a reason I was so drawn to being around women. I enjoy their company. But I couldn't do a long-term commitment."

Hudson sat back, processing. His perspective was changing, but there was still the twins. "Didn't you realize that every time one of your girlfriends left, the twins would cry? Each time, they said they thought she was going to be our new mother. I couldn't stand it. I didn't know how to help. They would come to my bedroom and want to sleep with me because they were so sad. I would tell them they didn't need a new mom, that they had me."

Putting his hand over Hudson's wrist, his father squeezed it. "I'm so sorry. I knew they were struggling, but I didn't know they went to you."

"They didn't want you to feel bad. The twins made me promise not to ever tell you."

Hudson looked down. "When Zoe left, I promised I'd never bring anyone around Charlotte who wouldn't be in her life forever."

Eyes wide, his father looked shocked. "Have you talked to the twins about this since? I didn't realize they went to you crying. After each initial conversation, Clair, Abby and even Monica called the girls. They developed friendships that they still have today." His face relaxed into a smile. "They helped your sisters with their first dance and prom. Even with the first year at college. When there were boy issues, they were a lot more helpful than I could ever be."

Hudson was confused. "What? Why didn't anyone tell me about that?"

"Because you had made it very clear you did not want those women in our house. I'm thinking the girls didn't want to upset you when they continued being friends with them. Not bringing people in and out of your child's life makes you a good parent, but you're not doing that. Being a responsible parent doesn't mean you can't have adult relationships."

A part of him was mad at his sisters, but they didn't know his secret vow not to date or why. "They still talk to these women?"

"Yeah. Till this day, they are in their lives. If you don't believe me, ask your sisters. Truthfully, you were just so angry when they were around that it was difficult for all of us. We were all trying to protect you."

The air left his lungs. They were trying to protect him.

"That girl seems to be a keeper. You're not being stupid, are you?"

"I'm not sure."

His father got up, then went to the door and opened it. "Your mother wanted nothing more than for you and your sisters to be happy. If that girl makes you happy, go get her."

"What if I love her more than she loves me?" Was that his real fear? Had he just been hiding behind his daughter?

"You won't know if you don't ask."

Heart racing, Hudson stepped out onto his deck. Which direction did they go?

"Are you looking for us?" Madison's voice pulled him to the left. There they were. But Abigail wasn't with them.

He ran down the steps and across the street. "Where's Abigail?"

"Margarita called and wanted to know if she would be able to help out. They've been slammed with orders. She went to the *panadería*."

"But we're going to keep Paloma." Charlotte clapped.

"Don't worry, brother, we didn't kidnap her. We're just babysitting her for an hour or two." Liberty grinned at him.

He looked at his sisters. "So you still have relationships with the women Dad dated?" Their identical looks of confusion answered his question.

"Yes." They looked at each other, then back to him. "Is that a problem?"

"I... no. I need to talk to Abigail."

"Finally." Liberty rolled her eyes.

"If you're looking for Abigail, she—"

He didn't stay long enough to hear the rest of Madison's sentence. Abigail had left without telling him and he had an urgent need to reach her, to tell her everything before another minute slipped by.

Hudson's heart was pounding in his ears, and his lungs burned as he ran. Cutting up from the beach, he hit the boardwalk. People honked as he ran. They were probably thinking their sheriff had lost it.

He had. His heart was in Abigail's hands. He couldn't waste another moment with her thinking she wasn't worth the risk. He needed to let her know she was. That he was willing to risk it *all* for her.

The bakery was across the boardwalk. He stopped at the curb, resting his hands on his knees as he tried to steady his breath. His lungs protested. Sprinting down the beach had not been his best idea.

Every parking spot was taken, and people were coming and going into the Dulce Panadería. After the week-long freeze, everyone was craving their hand-ground coffee and fresh pastries.

Well, he clearly had not thought this out. He stood looking right and left, waiting for the cars to pass, then crossed the street. It seemed a lifetime ago when he'd opened that door and saw her standing there.

He hadn't known she was going to change his life. He smiled. Change was scary, but it was good.

A few more people left the bakery, some waving to him. A couple of cars had pulled away. He paused in front of the door. With one last deep breath, he opened it and walked in. He smiled at the happy little bell that announced his arrival.

Abigail looked up from the cash register. A frown wrinkled her forehead. "Is Paloma, okay?" Emerging from behind the counter, she approached the front of the store, her gaze searching his. "Hudson, tell me what's wrong."

He was here, but now he had no clue what to say. He swallowed. "You didn't say goodbye."

She tilted her head, narrowing her eyes in confusion. "I don't understand."

"You promised never to leave without saying goodbye. You left. You didn't say goodbye."

Everyone in the bakery had gone silent. Josefina and

Margarita stood at the counter. Yes, he was making a scene.

"You said that when you love someone you should always tell them goodbye. Every single time."

Her eyes went wide. "I did say that."

The pounding in his ears was so loud, she had to hear it. "There are a lot of things I should have said to you on the swing. I lied. I wasn't sorry I kissed you. That was the best kiss I've ever experienced. I want to kiss you good morning every day and every time one of us leaves. But you have your whole life in front of you. I don't want to get in the way."

She smiled. "I'm glad you're not sorry. But all the other stuff doesn't mean anything if I don't have you to share it with. You make my life richer, Hudson, fuller than I ever thought possible. Stop being so heroic. Please."

He blinked a couple of times. With both hands, he cupped her face and pulled her to him. Or maybe she fell into him. He wasn't sure who went where, but they met in the middle. Their lips touched, and he knew it was right. Then he pressed his lips to her forehead, and everyone around them cheered. Pulling back, he kept his gaze on her. "I forgot we had an audience." He took her hand and led her out the front door and over to the beach.

Under the pier, it was quiet except for the crashing waves. "Abigail, I love you so much, but I need to know what you want."

"I—I don't understand this sudden about-face. Just this morning, you said all we could be was friends."

"Because I'm an emotional coward. I was afraid you would hurt me and my daughter when you left."

"Oh, Hudson. I'm not going anywhere."

They stared at each other for a long moment. "It's okay if you do. I'll still love you."

She cupped his face with her hand. "I love you so much. There are so many things I want to do, but I want to share it all with you. But are you sure you want to take me on? I come with a lot of baggage. As sheriff, should you be hanging out with someone who was married to a convicted con artist?"

He wrapped his arms around her. "Our pasts don't matter. It's what our future holds that makes you the perfect girl for me."

She laughed. "There is nothing perfect about me. I'm as flawed as they come."

"And that's why I love you. Will you be my forever girl?"

"I'm not sure I know how to be a forever girl."

"Then I'll come to Dulce Panadería every morning until you figure it out."

She leaned into his chest, her ear against his heart. "I love you. Everything I want is right here in Port Del Mar. When God put me on the road home, I was so scared. I had no idea how wonderful it would be."

"You woke up my heart. Thank you, love."

Stepping back, she looked to the beach. "I should get back to the *panadería*."

Over her shoulder, in the deep shadow of the pier, was a clump of pure, untouched snow. He smiled. Reaching over, he scooped it up in one hand and made a ball.

"Abigail."

She turned. Her brows raised in question. He threw the snowball. "Caught you." He tossed her words from the beach back to her.

She brushed the snow off her chest. "You did. You caught me." Tilting her head, she gave him a sly smile. "Or have I caught you?"

He gathered up more snow and she ran, laughing. He followed her. He would follow her anywhere.

Epilogue

Abigail shifted in the saddle. The chestnut mare underneath her waited patiently. From atop his gray gelding, Xavier reached over and took her hand. There was a shine in his eye as he smiled at her.

"Are you ready?" he asked gruffly.

"I've been ready my whole life." Excitement had her heart pounding in double time.

"More like your life got you ready for this." Winking, he sat up and adjusted the reins.

That was true. If her path had been easy, she wouldn't have seen the true gift Hudson was and she wouldn't have been able to bring what he needed to his life. Then there was Paloma. Her daughter was the true treasure. "God works it all for good."

"That He does. It's good to take it slow. Rushing into something never ends well. You and Hudson, you are going to end well."

Over the rise, the music changed. "That's our cue."

With a nod, she urged her horse forward and fell in step with Xavier. The breeze caught her veil and for a moment her vision was hazy. Straightening it, she froze.

Her lungs stopped working. Everyone that had become an important part of her life was standing and looking at her. Her lost family, her new family, and now her very own family.

Her new life was richer than anything her ex-husband had given her.

As they approached the last row of chairs, they stopped the horses and Xavier dismounted to come help her off her horse.

A couple of the Espinoza boys took the horses.

Her brother laid her hand over his arm.

She looked up at him and smiled. "Thank you for walking me down the aisle."

"My baby sister is marrying one of my best friends. My family is all in one place, safe and happy. There is nowhere else I would be today. Thank you for coming home and trusting us. I don't say this enough, but I love you. I'm honored you asked me." He turned to the east. "I think someone wants us to hurry." He winked at her.

She searched for Hudson. He stepped closer to the pastor and smiled at her. The wonder in his eyes made her feel beautiful and cherished. He was waiting for her and behind him the sun was coming up over the ocean.

When he had asked her to marry him, she knew it had to be in the morning facing the ocean. Just like the mural at church. Now here they were, close to the spot they were going to build their house on the family ranch.

A few people questioned the time of day, but Hudson understood.

He was going to be her husband and she was going to be his wife.

She squeezed Xavier's arm and nodded.

They stepped forward. At the end of the aisle Charlotte held Paloma's hand. Paloma looked up from throwing rose petals and seeds and squealed. "My mamma."

Standing to the left were Belle and Hudson's sisters. Next to Hudson was his father, Damian and Elijah.

He wanted Xavier to be his best man, but she said that was the only person that would give her away. The whole world faded the closer she got to Hudson.

His gaze stayed on her. They stopped before the pastor. Xavier laid her hand in Hudson's. Leaning in close he whispered, "I'll always be here. You're never going to be alone again, but now you'll build your own family." He kissed her forehead and with a nod to Hudson he stepped away. The rest of the ceremony was a blur. All she remembered was staring at Hudson, into his incredible eyes, holding his hands and feeling an abundance of love.

As the sun rose into the sky the kiss of the rays warmed them. Abigail didn't know what the future held but hope and love filled her now and she knew that would guide them on this new journey together.

Once the final vows had been spoken, Hudson leaned over to kiss her, and she reached up and cupped his face as his arms went around her.

The pastor introduced them as husband and wife. Her hand in Hudson's, they walked down the aisle, passing the people who filled her life with faith, love and joy. Leaving for Port Del Mar had been one of the darkest days in her life but now God had brought her into the light.

Hudson helped her back onto the horse, then swung up behind her. She laughed. "What are you doing? You have your own horse." She pointed to the one Xavier had ridden from the stables.

Reins in one hand, he held her close with the other. "Nope. I caught you and I'm not letting go."

* * * * *

If you enjoyed this story, look for these other books by Jolene Navarro:

The Texan's Secret Daughter
The Texan's Surprise Return
The Texan's Promise
The Texan's Unexpected Holiday
The Texan's Truth
Her Holiday Secret

Dear Reader,

Thank you so much for joining me on this trip to Port Del Mar. If you read the other De La Rosa stories you know that Gabby is the baby sister they have been looking for. It was so satisfying to get to bring her home. It took a little bit longer because we had to find the perfect hero. Those don't always come around as easily as you would think. But Hudson was there waiting for her and waiting for me to write their story. Elijah can be found in *The Texan's Secret Daughter*, Xavier's story is in *The Texan's Unexpected Return*. Belle and Quinn are in *The Texan's Promise* and Damian's is *The Texan's Unexpected Holiday*.

Not long ago, the whole state of Texas was actually covered in snow and ice for a week. I was driving from Colorado ironically, when it hit. Highways were closed; electricity and water were not easy to get. It was an incredible week beyond anything in the history books.

Writing about something that I had just experienced was interesting. I love talking to readers, so please look me up on Facebook at Jolene Navarro, Author, or email me at jnavarro32@gvtc.com.

Hope to see you in the next book. We'll be hanging out with the Espinoza family. I'm excited to get to know them better. They're a fun family.

Jolene Navarro

THE AMISH MATCHMAKING DILEMMA
Amish Country Matches • by Patricia Johns

Amish bachelor Mose Klassen wants a wife who is quiet and traditional—the exact opposite of his childhood friend Naomi Peachy. But when she volunteers as his speech tutor, Mose can't help but be drawn to the outgoing woman. Could an unexpected match be his perfect fit?

TRUSTING HER AMISH HEART
by Cathy Liggett

Leah Zook finds purpose caring for the older injured owner of an Amish horse farm—until his estranged son returns home looking for redemption. The mysterious Zach Graber has all the power to fix the run-down farm—and Leah's locked-down heart. But together will they be strong enough to withstand his secret?

A REASON TO STAY
K-9 Companions • by Deb Kastner

Suddenly responsible for a brother she never knew about, Emma Fitzgerald finds herself out of her depth in a small Colorado town. But when cowboy Sharpe Winslow and his rescue pup, Baloo, take the troubled boy under their wing, Emma can't resist growing close to them and maybe finding a reason to stay...

THE COWGIRL'S REDEMPTION
Hope Crossing • by Mindy Obenhaus

Gloriana Prescott has returned to her Texas ranch to make amends—even if the townsfolk she left behind aren't ready to forgive. But when ranch manager Justin Broussard must save the struggling rodeo, Gloriana sees a chance to prove she's really changed. But can she show Justin, and the town, that she's trustworthy?

FINDING HER VOICE
by Donna Gartshore

Bridget Connelly dreams of buying her boss's veterinary clinic—and so does Sawyer Blume. But it's hard to stay rivals when Sawyer's traumatized daughter bonds with Bridget's adorable pup. When another buyer places a bid, working together might give them everything they want...including each other.

ONCE UPON A FARMHOUSE
by Angie Dicken

Helping her grandmother sell the farm and escaping back to Chicago are all Molly Jansen wants—not to reunite with her ex, single father and current tenant farmer Jack Behrens. But turning Jack and his son out—and not catching feelings for them—might prove more difficult than she realized...

Get 4 FREE REWARDS!

We'll send you 2 FREE Books plus 2 FREE Mystery Gifts.

FREE Value Over $20

Both the **Love Inspired** and **Love Inspired** Suspense series feature compelling novels filled with inspirational romance, faith, forgiveness, and hope.

YES! Please send me 2 FREE novels from the Love Inspired or Love Inspired Suspense series and my 2 FREE gifts (gifts are worth about $10 retail). After receiving them, if I don't wish to receive any more books, I can return the shipping statement marked "cancel." If I don't cancel, I will receive 6 brand-new Love Inspired Larger-Print books or Love Inspired Suspense Larger-Print books every month and be billed just $5.99 each in the U.S. or $6.24 each in Canada. That is a savings of at least 17% off the cover price. It's quite a bargain! Shipping and handling is just 50¢ per book in the U.S. and $1.25 per book in Canada.* I understand that accepting the 2 free books and gifts places me under no obligation to buy anything. I can always return a shipment and cancel at any time. The free books and gifts are mine to keep no matter what I decide.

Choose one: ☐ **Love Inspired**
Larger-Print
(122/322 IDN GNWC)

☐ **Love Inspired Suspense**
Larger-Print
(107/307 IDN GNWN)

Name (please print)

Address   Apt. #

City   State/Province   Zip/Postal Code

Email: Please check this box ☐ if you would like to receive newsletters and promotional emails from Harlequin Enterprises ULC and its affiliates. You can unsubscribe anytime.

Mail to the Harlequin Reader Service:
IN U.S.A.: P.O. Box 1341, Buffalo, NY 14240-8531
IN CANADA: P.O. Box 603, Fort Erie, Ontario L2A 5X3

Want to try 2 free books from another series? Call 1-800-873-8635 or visit www.ReaderService.com.

---

*Terms and prices subject to change without notice. Prices do not include sales taxes, which will be charged (if applicable) based on your state or country of residence. Canadian residents will be charged applicable taxes. Offer not valid in Quebec. This offer is limited to one order per household. Books received may not be as shown. Not valid for current subscribers to the Love Inspired or Love Inspired Suspense series. All orders subject to approval. Credit or debit balances in a customer's account(s) may be offset by any other outstanding balance owed by or to the customer. Please allow 4 to 6 weeks for delivery. Offer available while quantities last.

Your Privacy—Your information is being collected by Harlequin Enterprises ULC, operating as Harlequin Reader Service. For a complete summary of the information we collect, how we use this information and to whom it is disclosed, please visit our privacy notice located at corporate.harlequin.com/privacy-notice. From time to time we may also exchange your personal information with reputable third parties. If you wish to opt out of this sharing of your personal information, please visit readerservice.com/consumerschoice or call 1-800-873-8635. **Notice to California Residents**—Under California law, you have specific rights to control and access your data. For more information on these rights and how to exercise them, visit corporate.harlequin.com/california-privacy.

LIRLIS22

SPECIAL EXCERPT FROM

LOVE INSPIRED
INSPIRATIONAL ROMANCE

*Amish bachelor Mose Klassen wants a wife who is quiet
and traditional—the exact opposite of his childhood
friend Naomi Peachy. But when she volunteers as his
speech tutor, Mose can't help but be drawn to the outgoing
woman. Could an unexpected match be his perfect fit?*

Read on for a sneak preview of
The Amish Matchmaking Dilemma
by Patricia Johns, the first book in her new
Amish Country Matches *miniseries.*

"I'm not easy to match, and I know it," she replied. "My
sister is a matchmaker and even she had trouble with me.
That should tell you something. Maybe it's why I want to
drag some *Englishers* into our midst."

His stomach dropped, and he shot her a look of surprise.

"T-to marry?" he asked.

"No!" Naomi rolled her eyes. "But next to a bunch of
Englishers, I'm downright safe, you know?"

"Yah." He wasn't so fortunate, though. Standing him
next to *Englishers* wouldn't fix what made him different.

"I'm joking, of course. But I do give that impression,
don't I?" Naomi asked with a sigh.

"What?" he asked.

"Of being a rebellious woman, of wanting to jump the
fence," she said. "I don't think I'm actually so different from
the other women—I just don't hide things as well! They're
better at keeping their thoughts to themselves, and mine
come out of my mouth before I think better of them."

"That's…a blessing," he said. At least she was honest.

Naomi put the pitchfork down with a clank of metal against concrete floor. "We're polar opposites, you and me, Mose. I talk too fast, and you aren't able to say everything in your head."

Mose met her gaze. "It's h-hard being d-d-different."

"Amen to that," she murmured. Then she smiled. "But a good friend helps."

Yah, a good friend did help. With Naomi and her wild hair and even wilder way of thinking, he didn't feel so alone—she'd always had that effect on him.

But she was right—Naomi was an example of why the *Ordnung* was so important. Everyone needed to be reined in, given boundaries, made to pause and think. Because if everyone just swung off after their own inclinations, there wouldn't be any Amish community anymore. Everything they valued—the togetherness, the simplicity, the traditions—would be nothing but a memory.

But looking at Naomi, catching her glittering green eyes, he couldn't be the one to hold her back. He could try, but in the end, he wouldn't be able to do it because she'd always been his weakness.

Mose felt his face heat and he wheeled the barrow off toward the door to dump it. She was helping him get more comfortable with talking. That was all. And he'd best remember it.

Don't miss
The Amish Matchmaking Dilemma *by Patricia Johns,*
available September 2022
wherever Love Inspired books and ebooks are sold.

LoveInspired.com

IF YOU ENJOYED THIS BOOK, DON'T MISS NEW EXTENDED-LENGTH NOVELS FROM LOVE INSPIRED!

In addition to the Love Inspired books you know and love, we're excited to introduce even more uplifting stories in a longer format, with more inspiring fresh starts and page-turning thrills!

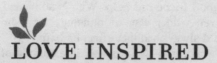

LOVE INSPIRED

Stories to uplift and inspire.

Fall in love with Love Inspired—inspirational and uplifting stories of faith and hope. Find strength and comfort in the bonds of friendship and community. Revel in the warmth of possibility, and the promise of new beginnings.

LOOK FOR THESE LOVE INSPIRED TITLES ONLINE AND IN THE BOOK DEPARTMENT OF YOUR FAVORITE RETAILER!

LITRADE0622